Gigi's Gift

A ROMANCING THE SPIRIT NOVELLA

CB SAMET

AVANTSTAR
PUBLISHING

Praise for Gigi's Gift

A ROMANCING THE
SPIRIT NOVELLA

GIGI'S GIFT

CB SAMET

One

S weat dripped from Rory's brow as he hung suspended above the floor, fingers brushing the priceless Irish cross. He strained to keep his weight evenly balanced in the harness around his torso. Beneath him, the ornate ceremonial cross rested atop a red velvet cushion on a pedestal in the center of a circular room filled with priceless antiquities.

Although it had been restored, the gold, silver, and copper had only a dull sheen and still bore the marks of centuries of survival—nicks, dents, and tarnished metal. The jewels had long since been distanced from the cross and traded across continents—scattered to the wind and thought forever lost to Irish heritage.

But Rory had located them through careful searching over the years. And he'd added them to his collection—some through outright buying, others more craftily. Like tonight.

"Steady. It's weighted, lad."

Rory glanced at the ghost of his distant ancestor. "*Sea*, Emmet. I'm well aware." His voice was irritable. He didn't need the ghost reminding him what he already knew in the middle of a heist. One mis-movement and Rory could set off the alarms in the vault.

He plucked the imitation cross from his waist and readied for the exchange.

"If you botch this an' the alarm's raised, the room seals and all oxygen's evacuated." Emmet's Irish accent was thick, and he spoke faster than Rory. His shimmering form was that of an old Irishman with whitish, wiry hair and wearing a beige léine—a long linen tunic that came down to his knees—over brown pants, and topped off with a brat—a smoke-colored, wool, sleeveless, hoodless cloak.

"Aye, you've mentioned that already." Rory grunted with the effort of keeping himself steady in the harness.

"I suppose it's not as difficult as the ruby you stole in Bangladesh."

Rory grunted his agreement. "You neglected to tell me that the little red stone was guarded by a tiger." Quick as lightning, Rory traded out the fake cross for the authentic one.

"I see some things," Emmet defiantly puffed out his chest, "but I'm not omniscient."

Rory pressed the button on his waist, and the electronic reel pulled him up toward the ventilation duct. As he rose, he tucked the twelve-inch ceremonial cross in his satchel.

"Well done," Emmet congratulated him.

Rory hoisted himself into the duct work before disconnecting the harness. Thankfully, the apparatus had held his weight. He broke down the equipment and stuffed it into this backpack. Pushing the pack ahead of him in the cramped space, he crawled through the maze.

He exited the way he'd entered at the basement level. Adrenaline surged through him, but he tried to temper the impulse to revel in his success. He still needed to vacate the premises without notice.

Before climbing out the window, he pulled on the backpack and wiped his brow with his sleeve. "All clear?" he asked.

"Sound as a pound, lad," Emmet replied.

When Rory reached fresh air outside the building, Emmet squeaked out an, "Uh, oh."

Rory froze. "What uh oh?"

"A raccoon triggered the south exit route. The guards've pooled over there. You'll have to go west."

"Where the motion-sensor lights are?"

"Aye."

Rory sighed as he flexed his muscles, ready for a dash through darkness and gardens. He would have to rely on Emmet's ghostly apparition.

"Show me the way."

~

ONE MONTH LATER

Gigi clinked her tall glass of lager to Lexi's. "Cheers!"

They sipped their respective beers, Gigi enjoying the thick, bitter liquid.

"Another week almost gone," Lexi said.

They met every Thursday to have drinks at O'Shaugnessy's and celebrate an end to the work-week—almost. Fridays were too crowded in the bar, so Thursday had become their celebratory day. Except, tonight was the first Thursday they'd seen each other in a month, owing to busy schedules.

"Your museum display is interfering with our Thirsty Thursdays," Gigi said lightly.

"I know, I know. It's been hectic, but it'll get better. We're cataloging display pieces on loan from a private collector.

Once I catch up, the hours will go back to normal." Lexi's gaze followed a man walking through the bar.

"And it's probably interfering with your love life," Gigi added, watching her friend scan the room like a feline predator on the hunt.

Lexi had full lips and long, wavy brown hair. She lured men with her sultry smile, engaging body language, and silky laugh. In comparison, Gigi considered herself plain, with short, mousy hair and solitary behavior, but she preferred blending in and letting her friend be the center of attention. Gigi rarely ventured beyond her favorite pair of blue jeans, a two-beer night, and watching her friend have all the social action.

"Oh, yes. Hottie at your six," Lexi said. "Don't turn. He'll walk past you."

Gigi glimpsed tight blue jeans below a snug T-shirt as Lexi's potential prey sauntered past their table on the way to the bar. The owner of the clothes leaned on the counter.

"Oh, gross. Gag." Lexi grimaced. "He just stuffed snuff in his lip."

Gigi laughed. "Why would you want to pick up a guy in a bar anyway. Who knows what you're going to get?"

"Would you prefer I look online?"

"I don't endorse that either."

"She says in her no-nonsense, authoritarian police-woman tone," Lexi retorted.

Gigi cracked a smile. "What about at work? You must have some selection of potential suiters at the museum."

"Um. No. Most are taken, and none of the ones left are personable. Besides, the problem with dating someone from work is that if something goes wrong in the relationship, I still have to see that person."

"Makes one night stands harder to pull off, too," Gigi teased.

"Exactly." Lexi wriggled her eyebrows.

"Fine. Bar," Gigi grumbled playfully. She wouldn't consider dating anyone she worked with either—not that she was in the market.

The bar had been a happy hunting ground for Lexi so far —if the definition of success was picking up a new man every few months. This wasn't how Gigi judged success, but the pattern seemed to satisfy her friend, who was certainly less lonely, or less *alone*, than Gigi.

Lexi took another drink before tossing her head back and snapping her chocolate curls off her shoulder. "You could live a little."

"Sometimes I want to. It's just this weird ghost thing."

"Which is in the past, right?"

"Clean and sober for five years now. I'm due for my next chip." Gigi raised her beer in a mock toast.

Lexi frowned. "Don't make it sound like a disease."

"It is."

"It's not."

Gigi leaned forward and lowered her voice. "If a person has a condition that completely paralyzes them and causes such profound anxiety that they have to medicate themselves when it happens ... it's a disease."

"You can't shut men out forever just because you used to see ghosts."

"You can't keep letting them all in," Gigi countered with a sassy smirk.

"I live life fully ... no walls, no boundaries."

Gigi didn't point out that her work as a white-collar crime investigator let her see the frailty of life and reinforced her belief in the need for walls and boundaries. Because she wanted to keep their celebratory Thursdays light, she didn't explain how people could be scheming, manipulative, and wholly untrustworthy.

A man approached their table holding a beer in one hand. He wore faded blue jeans and a burgundy collared shirt, and when he spoke, his Irish accent rolled over her, smooth as silk.

"Am I interrupting?"

"Rory, how are you?" Lexi stood with a smile, exchanging a friendly hug before drawing back, one eyebrow arched slightly. "Fancy meeting you here." Her tone suggested the encounter wasn't entirely happenstance.

He smiled back, bright-eyed and charming. "I'm fair. Can I fetch you ladies fresh a pint of gat?"

He turned toward Gigi, giving her a full blast of his boyish smile. She wasn't sure what a gat was, but if Rory and his deep, sensual voice was fetching it for her, she wouldn't turn it down.

Lexi said, "This is my friend, Gigi Montgomery."

Rory extended a hand. "It's a pleasure it is. Lexi has told me about you. You're a detective, right?"

Gigi stood and shook his hand, finding it warm and firm. Rory's eye contact lingered a little longer before he released her, but she didn't mind the long gaze. His strong, cleanly shaven jaw and thick, black hair were a sweetly handsome mix, piquing her interest despite her usual reservations.

"Care to join us?" Lexi asked.

"I'd be delighted, if I'm not intruding."

"Not at all."

"How do you two know each other?" Gigi asked, wondering if this gorgeous man with long, dark lashes would turn into Lexi's date for the night.

"Through the museum," Lexi began, "Rory—"

"Is helping with one of the displays," he interrupted.

Lexi regarded him for a moment but only smiled when Gigi frowned at their odd behavior.

"You're out of your Guinness. Can I get you another?" He gestured toward Gigi's beer.

"Yes, thanks."

He stood back up and walked to the bar.

Gigi turned toward Lexi with her mouth agape. "You work with him?"

"Yeah. He's uh ... helping."

Gigi eyed her friend, unsure why her behavior had turned cagey around Rory. Did she like him? She'd never mentioned him.

"Are you dating him?" Gigi asked.

Lexi choked on her beer. "No. No, definitely not. No fraternizing with co-workers, remember?"

Before Gigi could dig deeper into Lexi's odd reply, Rory reappeared.

Gigi thanked him for the drink. "Lexi tells me you're helping at the museum. What exhibit?"

"An array of Irish artifacts. Some from Cathal mac Figuine."

"He was a king, right?"

Rory arched an eyebrow—a motion Gigi decided should be illegal for a man as attractive as him. "*Sea*, king of Munster, Southern Ireland. You know Irish history?"

"Only a little."

"Gigi solved the mystery of a stolen plate from the Irish display at the Art Institute of Chicago," Lexi said.

Gigi swallowed a sip of her beer. "I learned a little Irish history in the process. I'd love to see the exhibit you're working on." She looked back and forth from Lexi to Rory to make it clear she was asking the both of them. She would never make a play on someone Lexi might be interested in dating—assuming she knew how to make a play, because dating wasn't something she'd had much experience initiating.

Rory nodded, brown eyes looking only at her and somehow making her feel she was the only person there. "It's not open yet, but we could go opening night, which is in three days' time."

"That sounds great." Gigi smiled, feeling oddly like this man's presence cast some sort of spell over her. Normally cautious and conservative, she was agreeing to an invitation that felt like a date. Perhaps she was reading too much into the man's magnetism.

They were interrupted when a tall, tan blonde woman strode up to their table. She wore jeans and a puffy white jacket with her hands fisted inside the pockets. A man with a long scruffy beard in tattered blue jeans trailed behind her.

"I heard you were back in the states." The woman addressed Rory in a cold, bitter tone.

"Hello, Ilene. It's been a while. Is this your new *ghrá*?" Rory's voice became deep and flat, nothing like the friendly tone Gigi had just heard when talking of Ireland antiques.

"Yes."

"So, it's official then?"

"I told you it was," Ilene snapped.

"No, you *texted* it was over, which wasn't adult behavior."

She put one hand on her hip. "Well, you dragged me to this dump, so now it's in person."

"So, it is." He kept his voice the same even tone.

"Where's my stuff, Rory?"

He withdrew a key from his pocket and handed it to Ilene.

"What is this?" she demanded.

"The key to a storage facility." He pulled a business card out of his pocket and offered it to her. "This storage facility."

"You put my things in storage?" Her tone was thick with incredulous shock.

"You were gone for eight months. I'd not a word for six of them."

"I texted."

"Like I said, not a word."

Ilene scoffed as she snatched the card out of his hand and spun toward the exit. She stormed out with the homeless looking man on her heels.

Lexi turned to Rory with a grimace. "That looked rather officially over. Didn't sound like there was much actual dating."

Rory—jaw firm and eyes narrowed—turned away from Ilene and back to Lexi. He nodded before scowling down at his beer.

"Oh. Handsome man at the bar just gave me the chin nod." Lexi stood, her attention derailed like a squirrel after a nut. "I *must* explore this further."

Gigi shoved to her feet and grabbed Lexi by the elbow. "Girls' night, remember?" She kept her voice to a harsh whisper as she glanced back at Rory who seemed to be studying the condensation on his bottle. "You're not leaving me here."

"Now's your chance. Rory's single." Lexi winked.

Gigi looked at her friend with a horrified expression. "His girlfriend just broke up with him. I'm not hitting on him now."

"This may have been the official break up, but it's obviously been over for a while."

Lexi pulled away, and Gigi was forced to turn around and acknowledge she was alone with a tall, handsome, and newly single man.

"Are you okay?" she asked lamely as she sat back down,

wrapping her hands around her beer.

He ran a hand through his dark, wavy hair. "Sorry for the public ructions. I knew the end was coming. It had already happened, actually. I wanted to force her to look me in the eye and act like an adult."

"Well, she looked you in the eye."

He chuckled. "Yeah, I guess I accomplished one thing. I'm more upset I ever dated her in the first place than that it's over. I made bags of it. I should've just let it go months past when she texted me." He slowly turned his glass of beer on the table in a circle with long, dexterous fingers.

"Made bags of it?" she asked.

"It's an Irish phrase, meaning I handled it wrong."

"From my viewpoint, she's the one who made bags of it. Letting you go was an idiotic move on her part. And really? That other guy instead?"

"Apparently she went on a medical mission trip and found her true love."

"Her loss," Gigi said, holding up her glass for a toast.

The corner of his mouth turned up.

> *"Always remember to forget*
> *the things that made you sad.*
> *But never forget to remember*
> *the things that made you glad."*

He clinked his glass to hers.

"I like that toast," she said.

He swallowed a sip and tossed out another,

> *"To a long life and a joyful one.*
> *Good health and a happy one.*
> *A cold pint—and another one!"*

She laughed, and they toasted again.

"In my country, we've quite an array of toasts," he said.

"Okay, my turn, Irishman.

> *May the winds of fortune lift your sail.*
> *May you navigate a gentle sea.*
> *May it always be the other man*
> *who says, 'this drink's on me.'"*

"Well done, Detective." He accepted the toast with an adorable lopsided grin that made her heart flutter.

Lexi appeared and looked back and forth between Rory and Gigi. "You're okay? I'm heading out with the snuff dipper."

"Seriously?" Gigi cringed.

Lexi shrugged. "Kissing is optional."

"Text me later!" she called as Lexi exited the bar with the man.

"She always leaves with someone." Gigi turned back to Rory, shaking her head in part amazement, part disbelief.

Rory arched his eyebrows. "And do you?"

"I have higher standards." That was definitely the reason. It was most certainly not because she feared rejection when someone found out her affliction. Or that most men were intimidated by her being a cop.

Rory nodded but remained silent. She felt like she was intruding on his post-break-up reflection time. She didn't know him well enough to offer comfort and needed to squash an absurd urge to take his hand in hers.

"I'm going to call it a night. Thank you for the beer. And the lovely toasts." She stood, but to her surprise he stopped her.

"You haven't eaten dinner, and neither have I. Join me for a bite?"

She considered the offer. Although the prospect of an impromptu date felt awkward, her stomach leaped at the promise of food. She considered her five year no ghosts mark, that she wanted to date again, and how Rory seemed the perfect next step. He was playful, easy on the eyes, and recently single so perhaps unlikely to rush anything serious.

"I'd like that," she said, feeling exhilarated and impulsive for the first time in as long as she could recall.

His phone buzzed. "One second." He looked her directly in the eye as if ensuring she wouldn't think he was dismissing their dinner. "I have to take this, and then we're leaving together." He answered the phone and left the table to go stand in a quieter section of the bar.

She softly strummed her fingers on the wooden tabletop and avoided making eye contact with any of the men seated on stools scanning the room. The difficulty of being a lone woman at a table in a bar was the cyclical offering of men to buy drinks. She faced the same thing every time Lexi abandoned her.

Despite her efforts to look uninterested, a suitor approached. "Can I buy you a drink?" His voice sounded overly heady as he sat in the empty chair across from her.

"I'm waiting for someone," she said.

"You shouldn't drink alone while you're waiting." He was probably her age—around thirty—but had an immaturity about him from the way he slouched in the chair. He set his drink a little too heavily down on the table, an indication it wasn't his first beverage of the night by far.

Gigi pursed her lips. "He's right over there."

The man smiled, but his gaze on her was a little unfocused.

"Anyone ever tell you your eyes sparkle like diamonds on the sea?"

"My eyes are green, not blue."

"An emerald sea," he amended.

She silently gave him props for the quick thinking, but still scowled her disinterest at him and the gumption he had to take a seat at her table without asking.

When the uninvited guest didn't move, Gigi reached down and pulled her Chicago PD detective badge out of her blazer pocket. She placed the polished brass in plain view. The drunken suitor's eyes went wide as he began to push away from the table.

"You're a cop." His voice now sounded remarkably sober in contrast to the seductive greasiness a moment ago.

"I'm a cop."

He slunk away from the table just as Rory came back.

The Irishman watched the other man leave before turning a pair of surprised sparkling brown eyes on her. "Was he hitting on you? I'd only stepped aside for two minutes." He sounded amused and impressed.

"He was," Gigi said. She picked up her badge and slipped it back into the inside pocket of her blazer.

"And that worked? You scared him off with your cop badge?"

"It's actually quite effective in eliminating riff-raff."

"As a repellent to suitors?" he asked, disbelief still coloring his voice.

"Only to the ones who have something to hide, or the spineless ones."

Rory laughed—a rich, deep sound Gigi enjoyed. It warmed her from the inside out.

"Well, it won't work on me. You've a noble profession, Detective Montgomery."

"Many men are frightened by the prospect of dating a cop."

"There you're wrong. Boys and cowards may be dissuaded from dating a female cop. Men ... not so much." He offered her his elbow.

Smiling, she stood and accepted it. She couldn't recall the last time a man escorted her, but Rory walked with her arm in arm from the bar, all the way to the restaurant.

Five years avoiding romance, avoiding ghosts, avoiding anything that made her heart race. And here she was—saying yes to a man whose smile already unraveled her.

Two

Rory held the door of the deep-dish place and let the warm, yeasty air roll over them. Checkered tablecloths, clatter of dishes, laughter loud enough to blur conversations—perfect. Casual. Anonymous.

The relaxed ambience would be a refreshing change in dating venue. He usually took women to nicer establishments, but higher tier places set certain expectations, especially when the women already knew who he was.. Tonight he wanted none of that. No expectations. No spotlight. Just pizza and a pretty woman who had no idea who she was eating with.

Was this a date?

No. Just an amiable bite of food with a friend of a friend —an attractive friend of a friend with a strong career, light sense of humor, kindness toward her bestie, warm smile, and affinity for a pint. Gigi had potential, but Rory wasn't in a hurry to start dating again—or whatever that had been with Ilene.

He would have preferred his public separation to not have transpired in front of the next woman he found himself interested in, but he hadn't known he would like Gigi when Ilene texted him, demanding to know where he was so she could retrieve her belongings.

As he opened the restaurant door for Gigi, her cheeks flushed, and he wondered if she hadn't dated in a while either. When Lexi had invited him to the pub, she'd coolly mentioned she'd wanted him to meet her best friend—an unsubtle set up if there ever was one. He'd fully expected to be polite, have a drink, and leave alone. Prearranged dates never went well for him—women often had agendas.

But Gigi had no idea who he was, and he found that incredibly exhilarating. He took in all of her as the hostess escorted them to a booth. Faint dimples gave her an endearing smile. Choppy brown hair she didn't seem to fuss over framed a lovely face. Her solid build had curves in all the right places. But she didn't flaunt her sexuality.

And although she'd apparently been out of the dating scene and a little uncomfortable with his attention, she wasn't meek or intimidated by men. She'd turned down a suitor most admirably without needing or even considering Rory's help. He'd never dated a cop before, but he was curious enough to pursue the idea.

Or, maybe he liked flirting with danger. What would this woman—and cop—do to him if she ever discovered his secrets?

They sat and ordered beer and a pizza, the smell of cheese and pepperoni filling the air.

"Does Lexi often desert you in bars?" Rory asked.

"Not often, but it happens a few times a year I'd say. She knows I can take care of myself."

"As a cop?"

"I've survived four older brothers, the academy, and helping her with a few ex-boyfriends."

"Oh aye?" He raised his eyebrows.

"She's dated some bad boys who needed more firm reinforcement about boundaries when the relationship was over."

The waitress dropped off two beers and two waters.

"And you do the *firm reinforcing*?" He wondered how firm she'd been with Lexi's suitors. Then he wondered how firm she would be with him if she didn't want to date and he became persistent. He felt tempted to push just to glimpse that "firm" side of her.

She blinked at him a moment as if trying to decide if he was flirting with her or teasing. Her vibrant green eyes reminded him of spring clovers.

He'd been both teasing and flirting—testing the waters, so to speak.

"I'm protective of my friend. I rarely have to get physical when I'm deterring men in their pursuit of her."

"Do you use your handcuffs, Detective?" He wriggled his eyebrows as he took a sip of beer.

"No." She cocked her head to one side. "Are you making fun of me?"

"Not at all. I don't envy the man who threatens your friend."

What would Gigi look like with fire in her eyes? Pure green flames burning hot enough to bring a man to his knees.

"Tell me about your work," he said. He'd only just met her and needed to control his rampant imagination before he got himself in trouble.

"White collar crimes—fraud and theft mostly." She drank her beer.

His stomach knotted briefly at the last word but he kept his voice even. "You don't sound passionate about it."

"When it's art and antiquities, I love it. Those cases are challenging and full of history. When it's credit card fraud or people swindled out of their social security check, it's a little more tedious."

"Rewarding though, I imagine."

"Sometimes. Often, people are dissatisfied with the speed of the investigation and want to know when the FBI will step in and take over."

"So, it's sometimes rewarding and probably rarely dangerous."

"Rarely."

"Is there some other detective work you'd enjoy more?"

"Like narcotics or homicide? No. I like the mental challenge of financial crimes. I guess I just want to cherry pick the more exciting cases most of the time."

"Mmm. The art and antiquities. Have you thought of joining the FBI?"

"No. But I have thought about the private sector. Investigating for private insurers."

"Ah. Then I'd wager you'd get high-profile cases. I'm sure it'd be more mentally stimulating." And the type of work that could have her chasing him one day.

"Yes."

"What's stopping you?"

"Comfort." She rolled one shoulder and shifted her weight in the seat. "My dad's a cop. I have two cop brothers and two retired military brothers. I know the government sector. I don't know if I fit in the private sector."

"But not all of your family is in law enforcement?"

She smiled. "No. In fact, my sister, Phoebe, is a treasure hunter." Her face brightened. "She has this whole Indiana Jones lifestyle. Museum curator by day, treasure hunter by night. Her husband is retired military, and together they travel the world finding lost artifacts."

"Fascinating."

"Phoebe has a knack for …" Gigi stopped herself and looked down at her beer. "She has a sixth sense about lost treasures." She looked up at him and blinked. "Enough about me. Tell me about your work."

He wasn't finished learning about Gigi, not by a long shot. Something prevented her from fully pursuing her dreams. Family? Finances? Something else?

"I'm passionate about Irish antiquities. The display Lexi and I are crafting will be showcased at the gala on March 17th."

"Saint Patrick's Day. That's fitting."

"We've a few Celtic pieces—a Celtic Christian cross with Celtic symbols and a gold bracelet of Celtic knots. There's a hand-held mirror of bronze with an inlaid floral design—flowers and buds. We've a set of old bag pipes—not as old as the Wicklow Pipes from 2000 B.C., mind you—but still aged. There's a huge cauldron carved with zoomorphic deities. We've a book of Psalms and a vase—bronze inlaid with a mosaic pattern. And there's an array of weapons—claideb swords, scions, boughs, javelins, and darts." The more he talked, the more he wished he was showing her the actual pieces rather than waiting on deep-dish pizza.

"Sounds amazing."

When the food arrived, they talked more about Irish history, and he asked about the cases she'd cracked.

After they finished dinner, they walked along Michigan Avenue. A brisk March breeze reminded pedestrians that spring hadn't quite arrived. Despite the cold air and growing late hour, people and cars still bustled up and down the avenue.

"I had a great time. Thank you for dinner," Gigi said.

Rory carried the box of leftover deep dish. "My pleasure."

"I have to work tomorrow, so I need to call it a night."

"Of course. Thank you for an enjoyable evening. My car is a few blocks away. I can take you home."

She pulled out her phone as her lips curled in amusement. "I like you, Rory. But I don't know you. You don't get to know where I live just yet."

He chuckled. He'd never had a woman insinuate he might be unscrupulous.

She opened an app and ordered a rideshare as the wind danced through her short, brown locks.

"I understand," he said, humor in his voice. He stepped closer, turning on the charm. "I'll settle for your liking me." He reached up with one hand and adjusted the collar of her blazer, not because it needed adjusting, but because the motion gave him an excuse to brush his fingers along her neck.

He'd wanted to touch her since the moment she'd smiled at him in the bar, and the urge grew as he learned more about her. His behavior, and the level of interest he felt so soon after meeting her, was entirely out of character for him. He had too much work still to do to entangle himself with a woman. And he had too many secrets to get involved with a cop.

She stared at him, a flush creeping from her neck into her cheeks.

He retreated a step back, not knowing her well enough to be certain if the pink represented interest or wariness. And he was advancing—at least in his mind—entirely too fast.

"To prove to you I'm a trustworthy gentleman, I'll forgo stealing a goodnight kiss." He clamped his jaw shut, surprised by his own words. She could trust him though. A kiss was the only thing he wanted to steal from her.

Did he want to kiss her? Yes. Just one taste to convey his interest, but he needed to earn her trust first. He needed her to trust him as much as possible, because she would likely be furious if she ever learned he'd omitted certain details about who he was and what he did for a living. Inevitably, she would learn his public identity. If he was careful, she might never learn his private one.

"Have I earned your phone number at least?" he asked.

She smiled. "Yes."

They exchanged numbers.

"Goodnight, Rory."

"Goodnight, Detective."

He watched her climb into her rideshare and leave but caught her glancing back from out the window. Ah, now he had confirmation she was interested in him.

When Gigi was out of sight, Rory's great grandfather's ghost, Emmet, shimmered into view. "Aye, she's a fair one, but mind yourself, lad. She sees what other folk don't."

"Are you certain?" Rory stammered, unable to suppress the surge of excitement rising in him at Emmet's words.

Rory had known the moment he'd locked eyes with Gigi —well, that sounded cheesy. He *suspected* she had certain uncommon abilities, but he couldn't ground his feeling in any definitive logic. And couldn't outright ask her. If he had and he'd been wrong, at best she would laugh him off and avoid him and at worst she would cuff him and haul him to the station.

"Aye, she's a medium," Emmet said.

Rory stuck his hands in his pockets. "Good thing you stayed hidden," he said, though Emmet usually did when Rory was around other people.

"What're you goin' to do about it?"

Rory walked toward his car. "For now, I'm going to bask in the knowledge that I've met another person like me, and we enjoyed a dinner together."

There was no rush in exploring their common ground in the spiritual world. They could slowly become acquainted over time, and he could see if she broached the subject of paranormal abilities. He wondered if she used ghosts in her work as a detective; it might give her a nice advantage—as it did for him.

Regardless of whether she possessed a connection to the paranormal, he was romantically interested in her. Yet, a relationship could be all the more fulfilling if he had the freedom to not keep any secrets from her.

GIGI ARRIVED at work the next morning still feeling elated after last night's dinner with Rory. They had exchanged numbers, and she'd had to resist the urge to check her phone every half hour to see if he'd sent her a message.

For five years, she'd been ghost free, and she was finally ready to see where dating would take her. She'd been surprised to realize she'd wanted him to kiss her last night. Maybe next time.

She tried to chalk up her bubbly feelings after one impromptu dinner together to a lack of dating in general. Surely, indulging these sophomoric feelings would only set herself up for heartache and disappointment.

She straightened her name plate: Detective G Montgomery, Financial Crimes Division. She spent the morning rifling through emails—so many emails. Spam for job offers, memos from administrators who seemed to have nothing better to do than write memos, interdepartmental shout-outs to officers recognized for outstanding behavior, notices for a form she needed to complete on a closed case, two week notices for annual compliance training, file requests from lawyers, and alerts from the Department of Homeland Security. The paperwork as a cop was never-ending.

The DHS email caught her interest.

`Subject: Flagged Arrival — Possible Alias: Felix Casale.`

They were notifying her of a passport they'd flagged on an arrival into O'Hare—Felix Casale. Well, one of his possible aliases. She leaned forward, focusing on the details of the notification. Everyone in white-collar crime knew the international art thief. And few missed the irony of a world-class cat burglar with a cat name.

In honor of the legendary cartoon character, case files were often named after the show's episodes—*Feline Follies*, *Felix in Hollywood*, *Felix the Cat and the Goose that Laid the Golden Egg*.

She rested her chin in her hand as she stared at the screen. Bagging the cat burglar would be a career maker and about as likely as her winning the lottery. If Homeland Security knew of his presence in Chicago, then so did the FBI. They could probably devote more resources than she could to finding the criminal. They also probably didn't have a stack of case files on petty financial fraud to wade through.

Besides, no one was catching him. No one ever had. The man might as well be a ghost since no one knew what he looked like either. When video footage or witness descriptions had been reviewed in the past, he was suspected of being in disguise—enhanced cheekbones, varying hair styles, different skin tones, and an array of accessories. The only general consensus from authorities was that he was handsome, of European descent, and had a gentlemanly disposition according to witnesses.

She composed a memo and made sure other detectives in the white-collar crimes division were aware of Felix's arrival before tackling the rest of her electronic in-basket.

When she finished sorting, deleting, and prioritizing email, she began working on one of the many fraud cases on her task list, making phone calls and booking appointments.

GIGI PULLED into her apartment complex and climbed the stairs to her home. After letting herself inside, she dropped her keys on the entry room table and bolted the door.

The day had been a long and grueling one, full of desk work. She needed to hop on her treadmill for an hour to create some mental space.

Her phone beeped with a text message.

Rory, *Can I book tomorrow night with you? Dinner?*

Warmth pooled in her chest. She liked Rory, and their conversation had flowed effortlessly. He asked questions about her work and her family with genuine interest.

Her thumbs worked quickly. *I'd like that. Let me know where to meet you.*

She pressed send and then wondered if she was supposed to play harder to get. But coy wasn't part of her programming. She didn't have much experience with this dating thing, but she also wouldn't pretend to be something or someone she wasn't—except for the ghost thing. She would forever have to skirt around that dreadful secret.

"Gigi!"

Gigi startled, dropping her phone. It clattered on the floor as a shimmering, translucent figure hovered in her living room.

She squeezed her eyes shut. "No, no, no." This couldn't be happening. She'd been rid of ghosts for five years.

"Gigi," the apparition called to her again—an ethereal woman's voice.

When Gigi opened her eyes, her heart rate skyrocketed. A

pale figure with long brown hair beckoned her, but the figure looked blurred.

Gigi spun and dashed to the kitchen. "Not again." She felt the familiar sensation of hyperventilating escalate as her fingertips began going numb.

Rummaging through her medicine shelf, she desperately sought her pills. Her hands clasped the orange, plastic pill bottle.

"Gigi, wait."

Hands shaking, Gigi opened it and slung a pill into her mouth. With water straight from the tap shoveled from her hand to mouth, she swallowed the pill back. Her heart beat so ferociously, she thought it might burst through her ribcage.

She sank to the kitchen floor, leaning against the cool, metal refrigerator as she tried to slow her breathing. Why was this happening? Why now? She didn't need any mental instability threatening to jeopardize her job on the police force.

"Gigi, look at me," the soft voice pleaded. "You have to help find who did this to me." A soft voice pleaded with her.

Gigi looked up and blinked through tears. "Lexi?"

How was this possible? Was she hallucinating? The shimmering vague form of her best friend blurred before her as the sedative took effect.

"Oh, Lexi."

But the benzodiazepine Gigi had taken wrapped its soothing limbs around her and coaxed her into sleep. She'd taken a full dose, and, even though she'd consumed a mild strength to begin with, she hadn't taken it in so long that the drug hit her hard.

Soon a dark, rocking ocean swept her into its current.

Lexi's haunting voice faded. "You have to find out who killed me."

Three

⤙⤚

Gigi woke to someone knocking at her door. She rolled over and blinked. Wow, she needed to clean around her kitchen baseboards. And she needed a drink of water. She smacked her dry lips together as the fog in her head cleared.

Knock, knock, knock.

"Gigi, open up."

TJ? Why was her brother at her apartment?

Gigi pushed herself up from the floor. "Just a minute!"

When she stood, she took a drink from her sink and splashed water on her face. Her gaze fell on the bottle by the sink, and she remembered seeing Lexi last night.

No. Not Lexi. She'd seen *Lexi's ghost.*

A wave of nausea rolled over her at the implication of what a ghost meant—the end of a living host for the spirit.

Cautiously, Gigi's gaze scanned her apartment; Lexi wasn't in her kitchen or living room. Maybe it had been a bad dream.

Maybe Lexi was fine.

But she knew better. No matter how many times as a child

she'd tried to tell herself the ghosts were just dreams—or just her imagination—it wasn't true.

She placed her bottle of sedatives away in the cabinet and closed the door on the disheveled medications—all standard over-the-counter pain and cold remedies except for her anti-apparition anxiolytic.

After smoothing her hair, she pulled the door open. TJ walked past her into the apartment wearing a scowl. It was just like her brother to burst in uninvited.

"You look like something the cat dragged in," TJ said. "If you already know, why aren't you answering your phone?"

"Know what?"

TJ picked her phone off the kitchen floor and tapped the screen. "Five text messages and three voice messages. So, you don't know."

Gigi clutched the edge of the counter top. "Know what?" she repeated. But she didn't want to know. Or at least, she didn't want her fears confirmed with spoken words.

"Lexi's been in an accident."

Gigi's world started tilting again, but TJ placed firm hands on her shoulders.

"Let's go. Your friend needs you."

"She's alive?" she stammered, hope and dread pulsing through her.

TJ pursed his lips. "Yeah, she's alive. But she's on life support."

With trembling hands, Gigi took two minutes to freshen up in the bathroom. She'd just finished brushing her hair and teeth when Lexi appeared in the mirror.

Gigi gasped, hand instinctively flying to a holster that wasn't there.

Lexi crossed her arms and blinked at her. "You going to shoot me?"

"Lexi," she began in a harsh whisper, "what happened to you?"

"I'm not sure. It's all a little fuzzy. Somebody killed me. I'm pissed off about it, and I'm wishing you were a homicide detective instead of fraud."

"TJ said you're not dead. You're on life support."

Lexi's apparition flickered. "Oh. That sounds encouraging."

"Maybe we just need to connect your spirit back to your body." Even as she made the suggestion, she suspected Lexi's recovery wouldn't be so simple. If her body was damaged to the point of being disassociated from her spirit, could she recover from that?

TJ's voice sounded impatient from down the hall. "Are you on the phone, because you can talk to whomever on the way to the hospital."

"I'll follow you there," Lexi said and vanished.

Gigi emerged from the bathroom ready to go.

"Need a purse or something?" TJ asked.

"My phone case has my driver's license and credit card. I'm good."

She locked her apartment on the way out. They took the stairs to the parking garage, walked to TJ's F150, and climbed aboard. Fortunately, he'd brought his truck and not his donorcycle—er—motorcycle. He wore a helmet when he rode it, but she still worried.

"What happened to Lexi?"

"She fell down the stairs at the museum last night." He ran a hand through his hair—dark brown and cut military short. "When Lexi's mom couldn't reach you, she called me."

"Foul play?"

TJ glanced at her as he drove. "No. Why would you say that?"

She pursed her lips. She certainly couldn't tell TJ that Lexi told her. As far as Gigi knew, she and her sister, Phoebe, were the only ones in her family who could see ghosts. Phoebe's abilities had manifested late in life, and now she used her spirit interactions to find lost artifacts. She had adjusted much better than Gigi had to her abilities.

"Guess it's a cop thing to analyze everything," she said.

TJ snorted. He wasn't a cop, but he was a Marine—a civilian now but no less punctual and tough. She briefly wondered why Lexi's mom had called him, but then realized her actions made sense. TJ was the responsible protector among the Montgomery children. Of her four brothers, he knew Lexi the best since he'd been closest in age to her growing up.

When they arrived at the hospital, TJ escorted her up to the ICU and explained that Lexi's mom had added them to the visitor's list. He waited in the visitor's lobby as Gigi went to the bedside of her childhood best friend, tentatively entering the ICU room.

She wasn't sure if Lexi's ghost was watching, so she tried to hide the look of horrified shock at the sight of her best friend's condition. A white hospital blanket cocooned around Lexi's body. She had a breathing tube sticking out of her mouth that connected to a machine in the room, hissing and clanking with every breath. Other lines and tubes connected her to monitors and IV bags, more than Gigi thought possible to hook up to one person.

"Gigi?" Lexi's mom was seated in a chair beside the bed.

"Mrs. Blackwell." Gigi's heart broke at the sight of her.

Disheveled gray and brown hair framed a weary face that looked as if she hadn't slept a wink all night. Guilt stabbed her —last night she'd been passed out on her kitchen floor instead of answering her phone. Now, she couldn't stay and offer emotional support because she had to find out who'd hurt Lexi.

She hugged her friend's mom. "I'm so sorry you're going through this."

"The doctors say there's swelling on the brain and the next forty-eight hours are critical." Lexi's mom began to sob softly.

"She's a fighter," Gigi said, not making eye contact with Lexi's ghost who looked away from her crying mother.

Gigi patted her back and took a step away from her. "I'm going to check on something at the museum for Lexi."

Mrs. Blackwell sniffed and pulled a tissue from the bedside table to dab her eyes. "Thank you for coming, Gigi."

"I'll be back." She hoped the brief visit wouldn't appear callous, but she couldn't stay.

When she left the ICU room to go back to TJ in the waiting room, she spotted Lexi's ghost pacing in the hallway.

"We have to find who did this to you," Gigi whispered as she leaned against one wall.

Lexi nodded. "That was not the sleeping beauty coma I pictured. Please do not ever tell my future dates I once looked like that."

"I'd tell you to get back in your body, but I think I need you the way you are to help solve the crime."

"Ooh. Crime solving partners, like Rizzoli and Isles."

Gigi arched an eyebrow, "Not exactly. That was a homicide detective and medical examiner duo solving murders. I'm a financial crimes detective, and you're a ghost."

"Just suck all of the fun out of it, why don't you."

"Gigi?"

She spun around to see Rory standing in the hallway. Had he heard her talking to herself? If anyone found out what she'd just seen, she'd be benched for psych eval. Rory's calm, compassionate gaze suggested he'd overheard nothing.

She wiped her eyes and said with relief, "Rory, what are you doing here?"

"I've come to see how Lexi is faring." He held a bouquet of bright yellow daisies, carnations, and sunflowers. He wore black slacks and a maroon, button-down shirt.

"Not good." Gigi may not have known much about the medical world—or the paranormal world—but having one's spirit outside one's body was surely a poor prognostic indicator.

"Have they given any indication of when she might wake up?" he asked hopefully.

"No," she said miserably.

"She'll pull through," he offered, looking at her with soft eyes and a worried brow like he wanted to give her a hug.

She wanted to take that unspoken offer, but she had work to do. "I need to go to the scene of the crime." She walked toward the ICU waiting area to let TJ know she was leaving the hospital.

Rory's dark eyebrows raised as he fell in step beside her. "Crime? I heard she fell down the stairs at the museum."

"I'm not convinced this was an accident."

"I see." His gaze turned distant as his voice sounded troubled. "I'll go with you. I can help you navigate the museum and make sure you have the cooperation of the staff."

She glanced sideways at him as she paused before entering the visitor waiting room. "What is your role exactly at the museum?"

"Like Lexi said, I'm helping with the Irish display. Temporary help."

"Okay. I accept your offer. Thank you." She pulled out her phone and selected her rideshare app. "I've arranged a rideshare to take us to the museum."

When she stepped inside the waiting room, she found TJ

pacing. Odd. He'd known Lexi for years, but his worry seemed disproportionate for his sister's friend.

When he saw her, he stopped. "How is Lexi?"

"Critical," Gigi said solemnly.

When his face fell, Gigi wondered if TJ had been harboring secret feelings for her best friend. And how long had that been going on?

She introduced Rory to TJ as one of Lexi's coworkers, and TJ seemed to shake hands a little too firmly, causing Gigi's suspicion about this strange behavior to blossom. How long had it been brewing, and how had she missed it?

"Lexi's mom is here alone," she told her brother. "She'd probably like some company. Can you take the flowers to her bedside? I need to go to the museum and check on something with Rory."

As TJ shuffled toward the ICU, Gigi made a mental note to ask him later about his feelings for Lexi.

When they reached the ground floor, they exited the hospital and walked past valet parking and a limousine and toward the rideshare pick-up and drop-off section.

GIGI silently worried over Lexi as she rode beside Rory on the way to the museum. He kept quiet also, as if respecting her need for solitude. But a few minutes into the ride, he placed his hand beside hers on the seat between them. She slid hers one inch over to rest her fingers on his. As he looped his through hers, warmth and comfort spread through her body.

When they arrived at the museum, he climbed out of the rideshare with her. He waited as she sent a tip through her phone.

Focused on her agenda, she took the stone stairs two at a time to the four sets of doors—gargantuan wooden gateways to the museum, which itself looked like a work of art with its steepled roof, stone exterior, and Roman columns. She peered through the slightly tinted window as she tried the door.

Locked. She knocked loudly.

A scrawny, balding man in a suite appeared. "We're closed," he said politely but firmly to Gigi through the glass door.

Gigi held up her badge as Rory leaned around to make himself visible beside her.

The museum worker's eyes widened. "Ah, yes, of course." He entered a code on a wall panel and pulled the door open for them.

"Thank you. I'm Detective Montgomery. I guess you already know Rory Dunnigan?"

"Of course, of course." The man smiled. "Mr. Dunnigan, always a pleasure."

Mr. Dunnigan?

Gigi turned toward Rory, who only smiled.

"I'm Theo McDermott, one of the managers. What can we help you with, Detective?"

"I'd like to see the scene of the incident concerning Lexi Blackwell."

"Incident? I thought the tumble was an accident."

"We'd like to make sure. I work in the Financial Crimes Division and after-hour incidents in establishments with valuable art and artifacts can be indicative of something more insidious."

"Oh, my." Theo took off his glasses and cleaned them with a cloth from his suit pocket. When he replaced them, he looked back at Rory. "We certainly don't want to overlook anything insidious. I'll take you to the location where she fell."

"That'd be grand," Rory said.

As they followed the museum manager, Rory elbowed Gigi. "You made that up," he whispered.

She put her lips together in the universal *shh* formation, but let her eyes sparkle with humor.

His smile widened.

He was correct; no policy or precedence existed that mandated launching an investigation every time an accident occurred, but she needed an excuse to visit the scene of the crime when no crime had been reported ... except by a ghost.

Theo led them to a wide, white staircase.

"This is the offending culprit."

"Thank you. I'll have a look around. If I have any questions, where can I find you?"

His eyes widened at the polite dismissal. "Oh. Um. Of course." He addressed Rory, "You know where my office is."

"Aye, I do," Rory said. "We'll not trouble you long. Ms. Blackwell is a dear friend."

With silent worry in her heart and determined cop in her head, Gigi scrutinized the stairs as she walked slowly up, Rory following behind. She ran her hand along the smooth rail, imagining fingers shoving, a body tumbling.

This wasn't an accident.

And Gigi intended to prove it.

Four

Gigi wasn't in the habit of bringing civilians with her on inquiries, but this wasn't an official investigation, and since Rory seemed to somehow grease the wheels of cooperation with museum management, she was in favor of having him with her. In addition, he had a soothing demeanor and calm energy she appreciated.

The man was easy on the eyes, but his presence would hinder this part of her investigation because she couldn't converse with Lexi's ghost with Rory in close proximity.

She appraised the broad stairs and art on either side—graceful marble statues of Apollo and Artemis. She appreciated art, which was why she'd chosen to work in the Financial Crimes Division. She might have considered a more adventurous job like her sister, Phoebe's, but crime-solving was in her blood, flowed through her veins—if such a thing could be inherited.

Lexi appeared at the top of the stairs. "Look!" She began doing backflips down the steps toward Gigi. "I won't fall down any stairs as a ghost."

Gigi shook her head. At least Lexi could joke about her

situation, Gigi could not. She knew little about the paranormal, but surely a spirit couldn't remain outside a body indefinitely. For all she knew, it might already be too late. She wouldn't share that fear with Lexi. Still, Gigi felt the urgency of a ticking clock.

"Are you bonny?" Rory asked.

"Yeah, I'm okay," Gigi answered Rory. She reached the top of the stairs, feeling a little light-headed at the thought of permanently losing her friend.

"I like to walk the museum at night sometimes after work," Lexi said. "The quiet tranquility is peaceful."

Gigi paced at the top of the stairs, trying to look like she was lost in thought while listening to Lexi.

"If I could retrace Lexi's steps..." Gigi's voice trailed. This part of her investigation would be easier if she could poke around alone and directly interact with Lexi.

"Right!" Lexi said, picking up on her queue. "My steps last night. I started over there—the Mayan Exhibit."

Gigi decided to physically trace Lexi's steps, so she quickly walked downstairs to the Mayan exhibit. Rory silently followed, having no trouble staying with Gigi owing to his long legs.

Lexi partly walked, partly floated over to the Mayan exhibit. "I adore the intricacies in Mayan art. The geometric shapes and elaborate headdresses are stunning."

Gigi noted sculptures and pottery made of wood, stone, stucco, bone, and fired clay. A twelve-hundred-year-old clay warrior caught her attention. His stoicism and generous nose made her think of her father. Stone art of skulls from Chichen Itza reminded her of how the ruins in Belize were said to be haunted—not surprising with the violent deaths that had taken place there—sacrificed war captives, ritual offerings during disease, drought, or famine, and sport fights to the death.

Gigi shuddered. Having never had any interest in entering ghost-infested places, she avoided any destinations rumored to be haunted.

Lexi continued into an adjacent room. "Then, I crossed through the African art exhibit. I came up the stairs to the Greek and Roman showcase. I wound through the naked statues and looped back around to the stairs."

As Gigi followed, she took in all of the mounted cameras.

"Then, a man shoved me down the stairs right here."

Gigi positioned herself where Lexi gestured. "Here?"

"Two more feet to your left."

"Here?" She moved left.

"Yes, but he sort of grabbed me by the shoulders and hurled me. He was strong."

Gigi spun in a slow circle, glancing at Rory who was leaning on the railing watching her. "This might be a blind spot in the cameras. I'll need to see the footage to know for sure. Maybe cameras caught him moving about the place."

"I saw him! I could pick him out of a line-up!"

A chill slid down Gigi's spine. If she lost Lexi—if the ghost faded before they nailed this guy—his face went with her. Gigi crossed her arms and bit her lip to keep from reminding Lexi that as a ghost, she couldn't pick anyone out of a line-up. And since this wasn't an actual police case, there would be no line-up.

Hmm. She tapped a finger to her lips. But perhaps she could use a sketch artist.

"What?" Lexi asked. "You're scheming something."

"We'll come back to that." Gigi's gaze slid to Rory again whose eyes watched her intently. She cleared her throat and stared back at him. "I have a process."

Rather than an expression of worry or angst as Gigi expected from someone observing her bizarre behavior, Rory sported an amused grin.

She swallowed her discomfort—and pride. She would solve Lexi's case even if it meant distancing Rory as she made herself appear crazy talking to a ghost.

"Oh, aye. I can see you've a process. Most unorthodox." Rory's eyes twinkled as he pushed off the railing. "Shall we view that video footage?"

He walked to her side and bowed an elbow for her to take.

"I'm on the job." She didn't want to be rude, but taking an escort down the stairs didn't seem like a professional course of action.

"These are the same stairs a friend of mine tumbled down last night. Won't you please give me peace of mind." He left his arm in position.

Feeling a little self-conscious, Gigi accepted. Together, they walked down the stairs. This close, she could smell his cologne—fresh and lively as if he'd stepped straight out of the plains of Ireland. His palm was warm through the fabric of her blazer, steadying more than her balance.

Professional, she reminded herself. *You are working.*

Her pulse didn't seem to care.

When they reached the bottom of the stairs, he gave her arm back with a pat as he turned to look at her.

"Not so bad?" he asked.

"I'm not sure I should answer that, as I suspect you already know how charming you are."

A wide smile lit his face. "You think I'm charming?" He offered his elbow back out for her to take again.

"Still working." She didn't accept the offer this time. She wanted to remain professional on the job, but she also liked his proximity a little too much. "Just lead me to the security room."

She wasn't some bonnie lass in need of an Irish escort. Great. Now she was envisioning Rory in a Celtic Irish kilt ... and nothing else.

"Mmm. Girl, you cannot pass this man up," Lexi said

Gigi shot her a withering look.

"I know you," Lexi waggled a finger in her face. "I know that look. Well, not this look, but the one before it. You like him."

Gigi turned her attention to Rory whose smile turned devious, almost like he'd heard Lexi. But that was impossible. Perhaps Gigi's expression of attraction had been as evident to him as it had been to Lexi.

"Security room?" Gigi prompted.

"Right." He led the way through a series of twists and turns.

When they arrived at a wooden door, he pulled a keycard out of his pocket and reached forward to swipe it.

"What other locations are badge access only?" Gigi asked.

Rory hesitated. "Everywhere. All non-public access points —vaults, employee lockers and lounge area, offices."

"So, Lexi would have had her employee badge on her when she was pushed?"

"Yes," Lexi said.

Before Rory could answer, Gigi pulled out her phone. TJ might still be at her bedside and able to sift through her belongings.

"Hey, Gigi," he answered immediately. "There hasn't been any change."

"I know," she said apologetically and then grimaced. She only knew Lexi's condition was unchanged because her ghost still floated right beside her.

"Are you coming back here?" TJ asked.

"Not yet. I'm at the museum looking into something for her. Can I trouble you to tell me if Lexi's work badge was found on her? There should be a hospital bag somewhere in her room with her belongings." She looked at Rory's keycard and described it to TJ, while silently noting that his said 'VIP GUEST' rather than 'EMPLOYEE.'

"Let me place you on speaker while I look around." TJ sounded distraught, more like a worried family member or lover than casual friend.

He harbored feelings for Lexi, Gigi was now certain. He'd never said anything, but he'd also rarely confided in his little sister.

She glanced at Lexi, who looked clueless—either not registering his concern about her or not worried about it. Lexi didn't appear to be hiding anything, but perhaps TJ had been. When her gaze drifted to Rory, she was surprised to see him looking like he wanted to hug her.

The crinkling of plastic and clothing emitted from the phone.

"I don't see a badge."

"Anything in the pockets of the clothes they removed?"

More shuffling noises.

"Chapstick. A receipt. And a five-dollar bill. No badge."

No badge.

Somebody had taken Lexi's card after she fell ... or before they pushed her.

"Okay. Thank you for checking. I'll try to stop by this evening." Gigi struggled not to think about her friend unconscious in a trauma ICU bed.

She didn't want to seem callous to Lexi's family by not visiting, but holding a bedside vigil wouldn't solve the mystery of Lexi's assault. And Gigi worried this ghost experience could play out any number of ways. Gigi could lose access to Lexi at any moment if she deteriorated or if she improved. If she lost ghost-Lexi, solving the crime would be that much more difficult. Again, she felt like she was working against a ticking clock but couldn't see the timer.

She pocketed the phone and looked back at Rory. "Surveillance footage?"

He nodded, swiped his card, and opened the door for her.

She stepped into a hallway with several doors and followed Rory to the first on the right.

He wrapped gently on the open door. "Mac?"

A lanky black man stood in surprise "Mr. Dunnigan. How can I help you?"

Gigi narrowed her eyes at Rory. First the museum manager and now the chief of security. People treated Rory with importance, as his VIP badge suggested, and she had the feeling he was more than just a casual colleague of Lexi's.

"This is Detective Montgomery. She's inquiring about Lexi Blackwell's fall."

Gigi held up her Chicago PD badge—a gold-colored, five-pointed star with the word DETECTIVE in an arch above the city seal in the center.

As Mac glanced nervously at it, Rory added, "She'd like to see the footage from last night—specifically over the stairs heading to the Greek exhibit."

"Okay-Okay. I'll walk you to the video room and we'll pull it up. I took a look myself earlier. I didn't see any wet spots or obstacles Somebody had taken Lexi's card after she fell... or before they pushed her."

Gigi ground her teeth. She was investigating a crime, and the head of security was worried about the museum being sued for an unsafe workplace. Without evidence and only the testimony of a ghost, she couldn't reassure him this was about foul play, not an occupational lawsuit.

They watched video replays for the next half hour, and Gigi's guess had been correct; the spot near the wall where Lexi had been assaulted wasn't in view of the camera, which made her certain the attack had been pre-meditated. Lexi came on screen tumbling down the stairs. If Gigi didn't know her friend languished in an ICU bed with her spirit skirting the line between life and death, Lexi's fast, slinky-like descent might have been comical.

"Wow," Lexi said, blinking. "Nothing graceful about that."

Gigi rubbed her neck. She needed to go over all the footage, preferably with Lexi alone so she could finger the perpetrator moving into his attack position. But convincing the head of security to leave her alone for a few hours in the viewing room when no proof of a crime existed would be difficult. The museum staff would probably want a warrant, and she had no way of convincing a judge to sign one.

Theo McDermott burst in, looking irritated and flummoxed. "Officer Montgomery, a word please."

"Detective Montgomery," she corrected him on a sigh. She glanced back at the security guard. "Thank you, Mac." She stepped into the hallway to face the music.

WHEN GIGI LEFT, Rory didn't follow. He wanted to speak with Mac alone, and the detective was more than capable of handling Theo.

Mac's gaze lingered on the doorway. "What's this about, Mr. Dunnigan?"

"Detective Montgomery is worried about foul play. As you can tell from the footage, it can't be confirmed or refuted. Ms.

Blackwell's employee keycard is missing, so that raises a red flag. I've six million dollars in artifacts stored in this museum, most of which goes on display at the Saint Patrick's Day gala, so you can see how I'd want to ensure there's not a thief behind this 'accident.'"

"Yes, sir. I can deactivate Ms. Blackwell's access. Then, if the key card was stolen, it'd be useless to anyone intending to use it."

Rory considered Mac's offer. Deactivating the access card probably was protocol and would set his mind at ease in the event someone was scheming to steal something from the museum. However, rendering the card useless wouldn't help Gigi find Lexi's attacker and wouldn't stop the offender from finding a new target.

Rory shook his head. "Rather than deactivate her card, can you set it to alert security the next time it's used?"

Mac nodded. "Sure."

"And can security then immediately notify me?"

"I can arrange that, Mr. Dunnigan."

"Thank you, Mac. I'm grateful." After Rory finished reviewing the details with Mac, he left the security room to find Gigi.

Theo McDermott stormed away as Rory approached. Gigi's cheeks were flushed and her brow pinched tight together.

"Are you okay?" he asked.

She jammed her fists into her blue jean pockets. "Sucks to have your fake investigation squashed before it's barely off the ground."

"I'll talk to him."

She flashed angry eyes at him as if to say she could fight her own battles. Perhaps having four older brothers created a defensive side. Or perhaps it was a cop trait. Either way, Rory enjoyed the fire in her eyes—probably more than he should. As a man with money, people often bent to acquiesce to him, including women looking for financial security. With Gigi not knowing who he really was, she could be herself—free to flash irritation his direction if she felt like it.

He chuckled, holding his hands up. "Or not. I'm here to help, not overstep my bounds."

She deflated slightly. "I know. I'm sorry. I'm tense right now over the situation."

Rory thought perhaps "tense" was an understatement but didn't say so.

Gigi withdrew her phone from her back pocket and looked at what Rory presumed was a text message. Her body stiffened in a way that made him want to give whoever sent the text a piece of his mind.

"I have to go," Gigi said. "Do you need me to drop you somewhere?"

"I'll be fine here. When can I see you again?"

She looked up, eyes cloudy with concern and whatever worry the text on her phone had created. "I don't know. Things are a bit discombobulated right now." She backed away. "Thanks for your help today."

He wanted to reach for her, hold her, and comfort her, but he didn't know her well enough for such an intimate gesture. And she might misinterpret such a thing and think he considered her weak.

Clearly, he was the weak one—he wanted to spend more time with her when they'd only just met. He wanted to help solve her friend's assault and give Gigi peace.

He watched Lexi's ghost trail after her. "Are you blind to the way that man looks at you? What was in the text? Where are we going?"

Rory shook his head with an amused smile as the women

left the building with their backs to him. Lexi was advocating on his behalf even though she clearly had more pressing issues, like who had tried to kill her and if she would survive another day.

At some point, he'd have to let Gigi know he could see ghosts too. At the very least, she wouldn't have to try so hard to look normal while Lexi was being her boisterous, distracting self.

He'd never told anyone his secret, and a nervous excitement filled him at the prospect. Would sharing a connection to the paranormal realm bring Gigi and him together, or would it destroy their chances at a relationship before it began?

If sharing the truth brought them together, it could change everything. If it didn't ... he'd lose the only woman who could see both his worlds.

Five

"Why am I receiving calls that one of my detectives is snooping around the museum asking questions as if there's an investigation when there is no investigation?" the Chief of Police demanded, looming over his desk and staring down at Gigi.

She had briefly gone home after the museum to tidy up and grab her gun before driving to the station to face the wrath of Theo having called the department. She figured the infraction would be worth a verbal warning and nothing as egregious as turning in her badge and gun. Still, she'd never been chastised for her work on the force, and the tongue lashing incensed more than intimidated her.

"I'm investigating." She stood stock still at attention in front of his large desk. "I don't believe Lexi just fell down the stairs, and no one can produce her museum ID card—which gives the beholder key card access to the museum. There might be a theft in the planning." Even with card access, there were still alarms in place, but a clever thief could bypass them.

"Good for you," Lexi cheered. "Stand up to your dad. Man, that look used to terrify me when we were kids."

"That's a stretch." Gigi's father scrubbed a hand along his jaw and up over his balding head. He looked about to tell her to back off her investigation when the phone rang.

After he listened, he swore into the phone. "Yeah. Okay. I thought the medication was supposed to fix this... Yeah. Okay."

He hung up the phone with tense worry lines around his eyes as he pulled his car keys out of his desk drawer.

"What's wrong?" Gigi asked.

"My brother's AWOL again. Third time this month." His brow knitted together as he white-knuckle-gripped his keys. "I'm going to have to put him in a facility—assisted living is not cutting it. I need to go get him." He sighed.

"He's at the North Bridge mall," Lexi said.

Gigi shot her friend an incredulous look.

Lexi blinked. "Well that just popped in my head. How do I know where your crazy uncle is?"

"I'll get him," Gigi told her dad.

The Chief of Police frowned. "I'm not sure where he is. I usually have to do a whole perimeter search, hoping I don't find him in a ditch from trying to cross the road. Last time he was found in a thrift store."

"I'll take care of it."

He eyed her suspiciously with hands on his hips. "Is this you trying to ease back in my good graces?"

"That, and I need to do something to keep busy if I can't work the case." She didn't add that, thanks to Lexi, she would be able to find Uncle Ken quickly.

"Okay. If you don't find him by dusk, we'll enlist more help."

Gigi left the station with Lexi's ghost in tow. She climbed into her blue Jeep and drove north on Highway 41 to The Shops at North Bridge.

The March afternoon was warming nicely. Along the road, harbingers of spring waved in the breeze—winter aconite with their little white flowers were already in bloom, along with blue, bell-shaped grape hyacinth.

"What's the deal with your uncle?" Lexi floated on the passenger seat. "This is really hard, by the way—focusing to keep inside your moving car."

"You do look a little glitchy. More transparent."Gigi shifted her weight in her car. "My uncle's had psychiatric problems for years, but was still highly functional. Because he worked and was wealthy, everyone just called him eccentric. If he locked himself in his condo for days, well, that was just one of Uncle Ken's episodes. He would bounce back. I say *worked*, but I think he *played* the stock market, since I'm not sure if such a thing is working or high-level gambling. He never had kids. After his wife died, his mental health took a dive."

Gigi parked her car in the lot and walked toward the mall.

"He's on a bench outside Nordstrom."

As she walked through the mall, it buzzed with energy—floors of glass-railed balconies, bright storefronts, and the warm scent of Garret Popcorn drifting through the atrium. Tourists and locals wove between kiosks and escalators, the polished marble floor reflecting a kaleidoscope of display lights.

She followed Lexi's instructions and spotted Uncle Ken sitting in striped pajamas on the bench. "Do so many people wear pajamas in public now that no one looks twice at them?"

Lexi scrunched up her nose. "Kind of. Yeah."

Gigi took a seat beside the man who stared at the shoe store in front of him adjacent to the department store. "Hi, Uncle Ken."

Lexi's ghost pseudo-sat beside her on the bench.

Ken looked at Gigi with glassy eyes before blinking them clear. "Oh, Gigi. Good to see you."

"Can I take you home?"

He didn't answer for a long time. Then, he scratched at a patch of unshaven gray sprigs on his chin. The color matched the abundance of peppered hair on his head. How did he have so much hair and her father had so little?

"She used to come here, my Moira. We had a net worth of six million dollars, and she'd shop at an off-the-rack shoe store whenever they had sales." He gave a slight, sad smile. "You should've seen her shoe collection. A closet full of them. I donated them all to charity—most of them barely worn—just like she asked me to."

Gigi took hold of her uncle's hand. His long, boney fingers felt cold. He'd lost Moira to metastatic melanoma, but she'd fought the disease for years, and the battle had taken its toll on the both of them. As for the money, she had no idea if that was truth or dementia talking.

"All these people I've seen over the years, and the one person who's gone for good is the only one I wish would visit me. I should be grateful. She's resting in peace. Still, the selfish part of me ..." his voice trailed.

"Let me take you home," Gigi implored, squeezing the hand she held.

"The ghosts say you're needed here." He looked back at Gigi with unfocused eyes and patted her cheek. "Aren't you just a princess? Since we're at the fair, you want one last ride and we'll split a funnel cake?"

Lexi crossed her arms. "Yeesh. His meds are definitely not working. You're one carnie short of a circus, dude."

"Who's your friend?" Ken asked.

Gigi's breath hitched as she looked between her calm uncle

and wide-eyed Lexi. Ken was making eye-contact with her best friend's ghost.

"I—" Gigi's world felt flipped on end, and she couldn't process what this meant. The only other person in the family she knew who could see ghosts was her sister, Phoebe.

A gunshot rang out, followed by screams.

The shot fired wasn't close. Other end of the mall, by Gigi's calculations.

"Uncle Ken, stay here."

As she bounced to her feet, she pulled her phone into one hand and Glock in the other. She dialed 9-1-1. "Shot fired. North Bridge mall. I'm on scene, plain clothes police detective." She gave her badge number. "I need all available units and ambulances." She muted the phone as she dashed through people running in the opposite direction of her. She kept her gun low so as not to escalate the panic.

"Lexi, can you get eyes on the shooter?" Gigi hoped there was only one and this wouldn't turn out to be some type of coordinated mass public shooting.

The ghost shot upward, faster than any drone. "I see one woman holding a gun standing over a man who's lying on the ground. Looks like he's been shot in the leg."

Adrenaline pulsed through Gigi as she reached the clearing and crouched behind a large decorative pot. She glimpsed what Lexi had seen—a woman in her forties with short dirty blonde hair, wearing yoga pants and a blue long-sleeve shirt. She held a gun. Revolver maybe; she found it hard to tell from this distance.

"Are there any other shooters?" Gigi whispered to Lexi. About three minutes had passed since she'd left the bench, and only the one shot had been fired.

"I don't see anybody else. There are a few gawkers. What's the matter with you people?" Lexi shouted, although no one could hear her. "There's a woman with a gun and you're standing around! Put away your video phones, and run for your life!"

Gigi took her phone off mute. "Are you still there? Good. Single shooter—blonde woman in her forties. Lots of civilians." She muted the phone again and slipped it in the back pocket of her blue jeans. She pulled her badge out of her blazer pocket and clipped it to her waist band where it would be visible. She didn't want her fellow men in blue to gun her down thinking she was the shooter even though their hair colored differed, but she also wanted to take the chance that this woman might be reassured by a cop.

A female cop.

Knees shaking, Gigi forced herself out from behind the pot and kept her gun steady on the woman.

"Chicago PD, ma'am. I need you to put the weapon down." She took small, calculated steps closer.

The woman's terrified eyes darted from the man on the floor to Gigi. She looked at the gun in Gigi's hand and the badge on her waist.

"I can't." Tears streamed down her face, carrying black mascara with them. "He's not supposed to be this close. He said if he ever found me, he'd kill me. I'm not going to let that happen."

"I'm not going to let that happen either," Gigi said.

"Shoot her already! She's going to kill me." The man in black slacks and a navy polo shirt clutched his bleeding shin as he writhed on his back.

"What's your name?" Gigi re-established eye contact with the woman.

"Darlene." She sniffed.

"Darlene, no one else is going to be shot today." Slowly, Gigi holstered her gun against the fear pulsing through her.

She wasn't wearing a vest, and her fate rested in the woman's hands. "You have a restraining order against this man?" She guessed, keeping her hands in front of her.

"Yes."

"Then he's going to jail. He can't hurt you there."

"Back to jail," Darlene sneered at the man.

"Back to jail," Gigi agreed, calmly. She stood close enough now that the two of them could talk in conversational volumes. "If he's been in prison before, then his proximity to you probably also violates his parole, so that will make his sentence longer."

Darlene's bottom lip trembled. "I don't know. He swore he'd kill me."

The sound of a trickle of water had both women turning back to the man on the floor. To Gigi's shock, Uncle Ken stood over the man, urinating on his injured leg.

"Uh, oh," Lexi said.

The man on the floor shrank back, horrified and speechless as Darlene gaped, a hint of amusement spreading on her face.

While every phone in sight recorded the insanity, Gigi used the distraction to step in and ease the revolver out of Darlene's hand. She slipped it into her jacket pocket.

"What are you doing?" Gigi hissed at Uncle Ken, looking around at the many mobile phones capturing video.

"You have to pee on it. It takes the sting out."

Lexi smacked a hand against her forehead. "Dude, that's for jellyfish stings, not gunshot wounds."

Ken shrugged and pulled his pajama pants closed. "I need to go wash my hands."

By the time Gigi dragged herself back to her apartment, she'd given a statement on the shooting, and endured another lecture from her father about charging in without backup. Both shooter and violent ex were in custody. Lexi's case, meanwhile, hadn't moved an inch.

Uncle Ken had been escorted back home to his assisted living facility. Gigi had made a mental note to talk to him about his ability to see ghosts.

Her phone dinged with a message from TJ, *You're a celebrity.*

He attached a link to a video. And there was Uncle Ken, urinating in public as Gigi gaped at him.

Another text arrived, this one from Phoebe, *Are you okay? I saw the video. Call me.*

Gigi groaned when her sister answered the phone. "Not the five minutes of fame any cop wants."

"What happened?" Phoebe asked.

She told her sister the whole story from Lexi's ghost appearing to Gigi's non-investigation to Uncle Ken and the mall shooting.

"I'm so sorry. How are you holding up?" Phoebe asked. "I know the ghosts during your childhood were hard on you."

Gigi involuntarily shuddered, trying not to think of the numerous counseling sessions, the antipsychotics—which only served to make her numb—and the endless worried looks and whispers of family baffled or frightened by her behavior.

"Mixed feelings." She uncorked an unfinished bottle of wine and poured it into a glass. "I initially panicked when Lexi first appeared. Now, my ability is going to help my friend. And earlier today it helped Uncle Ken and the woman with the gun."

"It's a gift, Gigi. I know my abilities have been. I met Oz

because of them, and now we're discovering lost artifacts around the world."

"Sometimes I fantasize about being an art investigator for a private company." She wondered for the first time if her larger ambitions were possible now that she could emotionally handle interacting with the paranormal.

"I know. You told me you were afraid to travel in case the ghosts came back."

"The last twelve hours has me reconsidering. What if the thing that wrecked my childhood can help me find stolen goods or stop thieves? What if they could help me the way they help you?"

"You'd be the best in the recovery business and a world traveler to boot."

Gigi sipped the wine, considering the possibilities of the gift she'd shut out for so long.

After saying goodbye to Phoebe, she pulled her shirt off and started the shower, needing to wash the stress of the day off of her and collect her thoughts.

She turned off the water and caught her reflection in the mirror—her, alone. For the moment.

Between Lexi, Uncle Ken, and Phoebe, it seemed the dead had always had their hands in the Montgomery family.

And now Gigi was finally ready to reach back.

Six

By the time Gigi had dressed in her pajamas and dried her hair, her phone was ringing.

Rory?

Despite her fatigue, she felt a twinge of excitement at his call. "Hello."

"Detective." His cheerful voice contrasted with the day she'd had. He seemed to say the word detective as if it was a term of admiration and endearment rather than a title.

"Not you, too," she said lightly, setting the phone down on speaker and running a brush through her hair.

"Beg pardon?"

"You saw the video. Calling to have a good laugh?"

"I did see the video." His tone turned serious. "And what I saw was an incredibly brave woman diffusing a dangerous situation. But what I'm calling about is to invite you to have dinner with me."

"Your offer sounds nice, but I can't go out in public for a few days. Not until the media frenzy dies down a bit." Not to mention she was well passed her adrenaline crash. She'd agreed to dinner earlier, but a lot had transpired since then.

"I'll cook you dinner at my place."

Gigi stared at the phone. Did all Irishmen skip the formalities and go straight to dinner at their place? "I don't think we know each other that well." That was definitely the reason and not because—with the chemistry sparking between them—she didn't trust herself to be alone with him in proximity to a bedroom.

Shoot. On the other hand, she did want to see him. Had she just ruined her chances because she sucked at this dating thing and didn't trust her feelings?

She added, "I'm sorry. I'm a little distracted worrying about Lexi right now."

He paused. "Too forward. My apologies. You're investigating more tonight?"

Gigi let out a huff. "Actually, no. Theo told the department about me asking questions at the museum, and I've been ordered off the case—mostly because there is no case."

"I see," he said in a contemplative, calculating tone. "What will you do?"

"I'm not sure, but her fall wasn't an accident."

"Then, we can discuss the non-case over dinner. The owner of a restaurant under renovation is a friend of mine. He'll grant me a friend and fix a meal. In this way, I'm neither taking you to anything too intimate, too isolated, or too public."

Her stomach grumbled its approval. She bypassed her unfinished glass of wine and reached into the fridge for a cold coffee. She would need the caffeine jolt to make it through dinner. "Okay. Text me the address, and I'll meet you there."

After they disconnected the call, Gigi changed into blue jeans and a pink sweater while intermittently sipping the coffee.

"That's what you're wearing?" Lexi appeared in her bedroom.

"Gah! No sneaking up on me on like that."

"I'm a ghost. It's not like I can knock or ring a doorbell."

Gigi pulled on her boots. "What's wrong with what I'm wearing?"

"You're going on a date with a—" Lexi hesitated, "—ridiculously handsome man who's cooking you dinner. You could spritz yourself up a bit. Brush on a little mascara."

"I don't pretend to be anything I'm not. If I wasn't starving with an empty fridge, I might not even go. Right now I'm a detective with a case to solve, and Rory might get me back into the museum. I can't swoon over a man while your body's in ICU and your ghost is floating around my apartment."

Lexi rolled her eyes with a playful smirk. "We need to work on your priorities."

"Oh? Are we going to talk about how I'm supposed to entertain the idea of dating someone when I can see ghosts?"

"It worked out for your sister. And I believed in your ability even before I became a ghost."

"Phoebe led Oz to an undiscovered tomb and exposed him directly to paranormal activity. I can't replicate that kind of bizarre encounter. And you've known me all my life—been a part of the little unexplainable events. No man with a rational mind could accept the existence of my curse."

Gigi slipped her phone in her back pocket and walked out the door toward the elevator.

"I happen to think your medium abilities are a gift, like Phoebe said." Lexi's voice was soft and sad.

"You were listening?"

Lexi shrugged. "What else am I going to do with my supernatural abilities but eavesdrop on my best friend?"

Gigi turned to look at her, flooding with compassion. "Maybe you're right. If I can help you—save you—it will feel like a gift for the first time in my life." She wished she could give her friend a hug or deeper comfort and reassurance.

"It was a gift today. You and I diffused the situation at the mall."

Gigi nodded. "Yeah, we did."

"Give Rory a chance. He might surprise you." Lexi smiled mischievously.

"That's what I'm worried about. I don't like surprises."

GIGI SALIVATED at the sight and smell of salmon, garlic, and butter as Rory placed two plates on the table. Fresh, lush, green roasted broccoli accompanied the perfectly baked fish. He set down two sets of silverware rolled in cloth napkins.

"This looks amazing." Gigi inhaled the aroma.

The restaurant he'd invited her to hardly looked under construction. The small, intimate place had been arranged so their table stood at the center, draped in a white tablecloth and adorned with candles, while the other tables had been moved to the periphery. Lexi had disappeared on Gigi's way to dinner, so the night belonged to just the two of them.

"It's a simple dish," he said. "I hope this doesn't seem over the top, but I thought you could use a quiet ambience."

"Everything is impressive."

"Are you on duty, Detective?" He gestured toward a bottle of Riesling.

"No. I'll have a glass." Gigi unrolled the silverware and placed the napkin in her lap.

After he poured the wine and sat, he raised his glass,

"May the luck of the Irish
Soar you to new heights
And the road you traverse
Be lined with green lights.
Wherever you go and whatever you do,
May the luck of the Irish be right there with
you."

She touched his glass to his, "You rehearsed that."

He winked, making her chuckle.

After taking a sip and letting out a small groan of delight, she cleared her throat and raised her glass.

"Wishing you all the merriness
and luck life can hold—
And at the end of your rainbows
may you find pots of gold."

"Marvelous." He clinked glasses, and they both drank.

After setting down the wine glass, she ate a bite of salmon, her mouth delighting in the savory fish as she closed her eyes momentarily. "Oh. This is delicious."

Rory smiled. "Good."

"No, better than good. *Amazing.*"

"I'm glad you like it."

"Love it." She tried the broccoli which had been cooked to perfect tenderness and buttery flavor. "Wow. Do you know how dangerous it is that you both cook like this and are single?"

"Is that so?" He forked another bite of salmon. "Go on, so."

Gigi swallowed and took a sip of her water. "You're exceedingly marketable. Good looking, good cook, friendly demeanor …"

"And?"

"Stop. You're making me uncomfortable," she teased.

His dark eyes shone with a mixture of intensity and playfulness. "But your cheeks flush adorably when you're uncomfortable." He dabbed his lips with the napkin.

"Hmm. Not unlike on the very public video today."

"That was your uncle? The man in the pajamas?"

"Yes. He'd wandered into the mall from his assisted living. He has mental health issues, although …" She thought about him missing Moira—how he wanted to see the ghost of his wife.

"Although?" Rory prompted.

She eyed him as she decided to launch a feeler. "He claims he can see ghosts. And the only person he wishes he could see but can't is his wife."

Rory swallowed a bite of food and set down his fork. "That's a tragedy." He took a sip of wine. "Ireland is full of ghost stories. The Derrygonnelly farmhouse. Corney, the Dublin Poltergeist. The Ghost of Castletown House."

Gooseflesh raised the hair on Gigi's arms.

Rory continued. "The interesting thing about most ghost stories is that there are only a select few who can see and/or hear them."

"Makes them all the more unbelievable."

"The people or the ghosts?"

"Both."

"Is that what you believe, Detective Montgomery? Or is that what you think you're supposed to say as one rational person to another? Do you believe your uncle is crazy?"

Gigi gazed into Rory's warm brown eyes—the color of decadent chocolate rimmed in gold. She was walking on thin ice and one misstep could spell doom. Did he believe in ghosts? Or was he bating her into admitting she did so he could dismiss her as crazy? The man didn't seem to have a mean-spirited bone in his body, but she'd only known him for two days.

Exhaustion—and something sharper—hit her. "I don't know what to believe." She set her napkin down on the table and stood. She needed to distance herself before she confided in him and regretted it. "Thank you for dinner. It was spectacular."

Rory frowned. "Yet, you're leaving in a rush."

"It's been a long day, and I have more work to do tomorrow." She kept a mental running list of things to do, including the sketch artist with Lexi and talking to her uncle.

He rose. "Do you need more help with your investigation?"

"I've been doing my job solo for years." At the hurt expression on his face, she added, "But thank you for the offer."

Before she reached for the door, he was beside her with his grip on the handle. "Come to the gala with me, Gigi. Will you be my date?"

She hesitated. "When is it?"

"Tomorrow night."

Right. Saint Patrick's Day, she remembered.

"Lexi—"

"If I could change the date, I would. But it's been set and announced months ago. Before and after the gala, I'll do anything you ask to help you find who hurt your friend."

"Okay. I'll go with you," she agreed, giddy excitement and nervous energy warring within her.

She couldn't think with Rory so close. Every time she tried to put a little distance between them, he pushed to close it. Was this the dating she'd been missing out on—simultaneously feeling too close and not close enough to the other person?

"But tomorrow," she added, "I need to work. Alone."

"I'll try not to bother you tomorrow. But won't you seal your promise to join me at the gala with a kiss?"

She looked from his eyes to his lips as the invitation hung in the air. She didn't have to travel far to reach his mouth. "Is that an Irish thing?"

"It could be."

What harm could come from one little peck on the lips? The man had arranged a private dinner after all. He'd made his interest known, and curiosity had her wondering what kissing him would feel like.

Raising to her toes and stretching toward him, she intended only a quick brush of the lips. His touch felt soft, but even such brief contact sent a wave of heat through her. Without lowering herself, she looked back into his eyes. They sparkled with desire—desire for her. But he stood still as a statue as if he knew she couldn't be coerced into giving more of herself.

She kissed him again, this time taking it deeper, feeling her body sing in response. In a state of euphoria, she closed her eyes and melted into him.

Their bodies pressed closer together as the kiss deepened, but he forced nothing, letting her set the pace of their exploration as he settled his hands on her hips.

She took a step back, touching fingers to her tender lips in surprise as her body felt shocked by sensations she'd never experienced with a single kiss.

"I should go." Breathless, her voice was barely a whisper.

He opened the door for her, looking dazed as he spoke in a low, husky voice, "Aye, you should."

· · ·

Rory let the restaurant door close as Gigi left. He'd been thunderstruck by her gentle kiss.

"That was a home run. Way to go, Romeo." Lexi appeared beside him, watching Gigi walk out of sight toward her car.

"I'm glad you think so. Parts of me wanted to do a whole lot more than kiss her." As such, he had to agree with Gigi's statement that she should go.

Lexi gaped at him. "You can see me?"

"Aye." He gave her a small, rueful smile. "I'm sorry about your fall, Lexi. I do hope we can catch whoever did this to you."

"All this time you could see me? You have to tell Gigi."

"Do I now? I've actually been trying to figure out how to work that into a conversation. It's a little more challenging than you might think. She's quite good at protecting her secrets."

"With good reason," Lexi scoffed. "She grew up thinking she was out of her mind unstable. She could see and hear ghosts when no one else could. Only Phoebe and I understood her. Or tried to. And even we didn't wholly believe in the ghost thing, but we knew she wasn't crazy. She tried to get help—you know, psychiatric help—without actually ever letting on that she could see and hear ghosts." Lexi sighed. "I shouldn't even be telling you any of this. She should be the one to tell you."

"I've never met anyone like me. I'm anxious to tell her, but it feels like a fragile thing—like fired clay pottery from the Neolithic period that might slip through my fingers and shatter. I don't want to do it the wrong way. I don't want to lose her, which sounds absurd to say aloud when we've only just met. There's a future between us, but one wrong step ..." his voice trailed off.

"So, stop keeping secrets. She's a detective. She's probably already figured out you're holding back information."

"You're referring to who I am."

"Yeah, Mr. Billion-dollar-antiquities-dealer who's pretending he's just an average Joe."

Rory took a heavy breath and began clearing the dishes off the table. Little did Lexi know that was only the half of it. "I found her treatment of me refreshing. She doesn't have an agenda, and I seldom interact with people who haven't one."

"You won't find any hidden agendas from her. Ever. But if you keep secrets from her, then you might destroy your chances with her when she does find out."

He drank the last of his wine before placing the glass by the sink. "I'll tell her. Actually, I've every intention of telling her, but I need to work out the logistics of how and when. After everything she went through today, dinner wasn't the right time."

"Judging by the way your face looked after that kiss, you have a lot of other intentions too."

"Oh aye, I surely do." He huffed a soft laugh. "As her best friend, will you grant me your blessin' to court her?"

Lexi snorted. "I guess this is the part where I threaten you bodily harm if you break her heart, but I see that lost puppy dog look in your eyes. Gigi's put up so many walls thinking she was mentally unfit to love anyone that I hope she's not the one who breaks your heart."

Seven

The next morning, Gigi went to Aurora Acres retirement home. Uncle Ken had been at the facility for six months, and shame washed over her as she realized that she hadn't visited in all that time. Prior to his relocation, she usually saw him at birthdays and holidays—up until he lost his wife and seemed to lose his way.

She braced herself for a sterile facility filled with delirious captives living out the last of their days slouched in wheel-chairs or drooling near windows. Instead she found a variety of active residents engaged in an assortment of activities. Inside, residents crowded chess boards and card tables. Outside, a few swatted shuttlecocks over a badminton net while others strolled the path, bird-watching.

Sprigs of green broke the surface of the dark soil lining the walls of the activity center and the walkways outside, and she suspected the area would be adorned with colorful flowers next month.

Gigi found her uncle playing *Fur Elise* at a piano. Warm memories of him creating beautiful music during the holidays flooded her. She recalled how eclectic he'd been—piano, violin, sculpting, and painting.

She sat beside him on the bench as he played. "I remember your fingers dancing along the keys while Aunt Moira sang. She had a beautiful voice."

"I remember you being our most captive audience, Gigi."

"My favorite is *Leaving on a Jet Plane*."

She recalled Uncle Ken's home always being a quiet place of solitude. No ghosts, no spirits, no voices. Their music chased away all her fears and worries about being different.

He stopped playing and turned toward her. "Did you want to leave on a jet plane?"

"No, nothing like that. I had a loving family and friends. I just romanticized the idea of someone waiting for the other."

"It's even more romantic when they join you on those trips—those adventures—rather than staying behind."

"Is that what you and Aunt Moira did? Travel together?"

"Everything together."

"I'm sure she'll wait for you for the next adventure."

Sorrow tainted the edges of his smile. "When are you going to begin adventures of your own?"

She ran fingers along the piano keys, thinking of how she'd cocooned herself in her job and apartment, always staying in the confines of her comfort zone. "Seems I'm starting now. I'm not afraid of ghosts for the first time in my life. I'm not crazy."

"Oh." He chuckled softly. "We're all a little crazy. But your abilities can be an opportunity."

She nudged his elbow. "Like you and the stock market? This is a pretty posh place. You even have ball boys for badminton. I've seen worse vacation getaways."

"You haven't seen the half of it—indoor bowling and golf range."

"Maybe I'll come back next weekend and we can bowl for an afternoon."

"I'd like that."

"For now, I need to solve the mystery of who pushed my friend down a set of stairs and why."

"I'm sorry about Lexi. Such a sweet girl."

"Well, she's not dead. At least not yet. She's in a coma—or something. I don't know how to reconnect her."

"She'll be okay."

Gigi tried to read his expression. Was he saying that body and spirit would merge and she would survive her injuries or that her spirit would move on and find peace as her body failed? She was afraid to ask for clarification.

"Can I come back sometime if I need to talk more about the ghosts? I don't know much about the paranormal."

He patted her leg. "Anytime, Gigi. Anytime."

"Can I ask for one more favor? I need someone to sketch the face of the man who pushed Lexi down the flight of stairs."

He nodded as he played *Leaving on a Jet Plane*. "For a price," he said lightly. "You break me out of this joint for half a day. But I have to be back by five thirty. It's pistachio ice cream night."

RORY SPENT the morning dealing with his usual business affairs. He balanced accounts and responded to emails. Although his real passion was finding Irish artifacts, he often discovered other pottery, weapons, jewelry, or trinkets belonging to other countries. The sale of these supported his Irish endeavors.

Emmet flickered into the room.

"Grandfather," Rory greeted him.

"While you've been playin' on that electronic toy, I've been locating our next treasure."

Rory leaned back in his chair and gave the ghost an amused shake of his head. "Playing on this toy is what pays our expenses in order to find the next treasure."

Emmet grunted as if to imply he did all the heavy lifting of their duo. "Collar of a knight of the Order of St. Patrick," he announced, puffing out his chest and hiking his britches higher.

Rory let out a low whistle. Collars were ornate chains worn around the neck as symbols of chivalrous orders. A collar of a knight of the Order of St. Patrick would be made of pieces of gold interlaced with vitreous enamel twisted in small Celtic symbols. A badge hung down in front—often a star, cross, crown, or inlaid jewel.

"Where is it?" Rory asked.

"Disassembled pieces are scattered in Berlin, Dubai, and Shanghai."

Rory envisioned the undertaking with rich anticipation. Probably no one with pieces of the collar even realized what they possessed. If he could gather them all, he would have an amazing new display for his next museum showcase and fund raiser.

"Grand." He pushed up from his seat, stretched, and checked his watch. "We can begin after the gala. I need to see the collection safely back to Dublin."

Rory picked up his phone off the desk and texted Gigi, *Lunch?*

"Didn't you promise to try not to distract her today?" Emmet said.

"I made it all the way until noon."

"I bring you news about a collar of a knight of the Order of St. Patrick, and you're breakin' for lunch with a woman?"

"I can't fly off to another country with the gala tonight—" the gala where the cross he'd "acquired" several months ago along with other priceless pieces would be on display, "—and we can plan our trip next week. Today, I'd like to enjoy a meal with a beautiful woman. I intend to tell her the truth about me."

Emmet crossed his arms. "She's mucking up your priorities."

Rory chuckled. "I disagree. Now, if you'd appeared here to tell me you'd found the Irish Crown Jewels, I might drop everything."

The jewels had been stolen in 1907 and never recovered. Whenever his grandfather's ego swelled at his latest find, Rory could humble him by mentioning the elusive crown jewels.

Emmet scowled and vanished.

Rory grinned. Their running playful contention also served as a way for Rory to reclaim time to himself.

Gigi texted back, *What is it with you and meals? Is that an Irish thing?*

Rory smiled as he replied, *It's a time of day thing. But I'll settle for coffee if you're not hungry.*

Gigi, *Are you going to clear out the whole joint? Just you and me?*

Rory, *if you so desire.*

He waited long moments for her reply. She texted him an address. *Bring coffee.*

His heart skipped a beat, feeling elation and dread at his plans to tell her the truth. They weren't going to meet at her place—or his—so he gauged that trust might still be an issue. He could accept her caution. Neutral territory would perhaps be better when he told her who and what he was.

Rory, *Thirty minutes ok?*
Gigi, *Perfect.*

TWENTY-FIVE MINUTES LATER, Rory stepped out of his chauffeured black Lincoln Continental with coffees in hand.

"Thanks, William. I don't know if I'll be a few minutes or a few hours."

"I'll be here, sir."

Rory approached the large three-story home, admiring the slate stone exterior and three gables with jutting dormers. It had three dormant chimneys and two second floor balconies.

Gigi wore blue jeans with her work boots and a snug fitting burgundy sweater topped with a navy-blue blazer. Her hair was its usual choppy locks with a slight wave. A man in baggy khaki slacks and a wool coat over a white button-down shirt stood beside her. He had frayed, wiry gray hair and an uneven beard in need of a shave.

Rory handed Gigi a cup of coffee. Lexi had been kind enough to make an appearance at the coffee shop and let him know exactly what type Gigi liked—splash of cream and one packet of sugar.

"Splendid house you have here," Rory said to the pair of them.

"Rory, this is my Uncle Ken. This is his place ... or one of them."

Rory extended his hand. "Mr. Montgomery, I recognize you from the mall footage with Gigi the other day."

The man smiled. "That was just a bit of fun. My connection to reality isn't what it used to be. Please, call me Ken."

Gigi sipped her coffee and eyed Rory suspiciously, probably wondering how he knew her beverage preference.

"Should we all go inside?" Gigi asked Ken.

"First," Rory began quickly, "I need to make a confession. I haven't told you who I am."

Gigi arched an eyebrow. "You are *the* Rory Dunnigan. Irish antiquities, real estate, and philanthropy."

Rory pursed his lips. "How long have you known?"

"I looked you up this morning after our dinner. Something seemed off. Lexi acted strange when we first met at the bar, so did the museum manager and security detail. And then you rent out the entire restaurant for one dinner."

"I didn't lie about that. The owner is a friend of mine, and it was closed for renovations. I know I misled you into thinking I was just another museum employee, but I wanted to enjoy someone not knowing the public side of me. I liked being just Rory and Gigi."

Gigi chuckled. "Relax, Irishman. I understand why you did it. I'm not upset. Everybody has secrets. Nobody knows all of anybody, especially not after just three days. We all omit things about who we are. You never lied, and there is a difference between lying and omission."

"You're not upset with me then?"

"I'm not upset with you." She smiled, but it was frayed at the periphery with that sadness. "I'm just not sure how compatible a cop and a man of your public stature are."

Rory grinned. She was giving real consideration to a relationship with him, even if her initial reaction was one of doubt. He could navigate the tentative waters of doubt. But first Gigi needed one more piece of information.

"There's one more thing you need to know about me. I'm also a medium."

GIGI STOPPED MIDWAY before taking another sip of her

coffee and stared at Rory. His words dropped like a stone in deep water.

"I beg your pardon?" Surely, she hadn't heard him correctly.

Ken blinked.

"I realized you could see and hear ghosts when I saw you talking to Lexi in the hospital."

Gigi cast him a wary glance as her heart kicked into second gear.

"You were conversing with the ghost of Lexi standing in the hallway outside the room of the unconscious flesh and blood version. I thought about telling you at the museum when you were trying so hard not to appear to be interacting with her, but I didn't want to interfere with your investigation."

"And dinner?"

He looked her directly in the eyes. "Dinner was wonderful. I wasn't ready to see you look at me this way. Like I can't be trusted."

Her brow furrowed and her world tilted on its axis. Rory could see ghosts?

He said, "Lexi, won't you be a dear and show yourself."

When Lexi appeared, Gigi stood frozen still without looking at the apparition of her friend. For years she'd been the only one in the room reacting to thin air. Now someone else was calling her ghost in like it was the most natural thing in the world.

"Hi. It's true." Lexi waved. "Rory can see me. I told him exactly what to put in your coffee—cause I'm a good friend like that. And I'm amazing for bringing the two of you together." She looked back and forth between Rory and Gigi who still locked gazes. "Okay. Enough about me. Back to my case.

Gigi, you promised me a sketch artist, and Uncle Ken is ready."

Gigi turned slowly to look at Lexi, her mind still searching for something to ground her. "Ken?"

"I've got a room in this house with everything I need to render a sketch." He started walking toward the house and then added, "As long as you get me back to the facility by dinner. It's pistachio ice cream night."

Since he'd mentioned that twice now, she wondered how incredible that ice cream must be.

Rory picked up his pace to walk beside Gigi as he wore an expression of worry.

"What's she wearing?" Gigi asked him.

Ahead of them, Lexi glided beside Gigi's uncle.

"Black slacks and a black sweater. Sort of a sparkly thing with frayed edges."

Gigi sucked in a sharp breath.

They walked along the marble floor, under a chandelier in the foyer, and toward an open door past a large dining room on the right.

"I can't believe it. I've never met anyone other than Ken and my sister who—" She hesitated.

"I've never met *anyone* like me," Rory said.

Lexi and Ken entered the art room, but Gigi hung back with Rory.

"It's a lot to process," she said.

He placed a hand on her chin to gently turn her face toward him, searching her expression. "In a good way?"

His touch anchored her to solid ground, and her surroundings stopped their faint swirl, changing from a Van Gough painting to a crisp Raphael.

"How are you so calm talking about ghosts?" Her experiences with the paranormal growing up had been difficult, to say the least.

He dropped his hand but stayed close, crowding her space. "Irish culture's a bit different than American. People talk about ghosts, even though most've never truly seen them. But because they're ingrained in our culture, we're not thought of as crazy for mentioning them—though I did learn to be discreet about it after I chased off a few nannies growing up. I read every book I could about the paranormal to understand my purpose."

"Purpose?"

"Ghosts help me find lost Irish relics—Irish heritage. They've been the key to my success. The same way your sister uses their help to find her lost treasures."

"Lexi told you that?"

"Aye, she did."

Her eyes lost focus as she stared into the art room. Ken was drawing an enormous face on a four-foot canvas using a thick piece of charcoal. If Lexi corrected something, he smeared it with the side of his hand and kept going.

Rory continued, "This doesn't change the fact that I want to take you to the gala tonight or that I want to date you. I hope you feel the same."

"Touch me again."

Hesitantly, he placed his hands on her arms.

She swallowed. "It's like I'm lost in between the world of the living and the spiritual—floating adrift. When you touch me, you ground me." She shook her head, feeling the foolish sentimentality of her words. When she moved to take a step back, he held her in place.

His thumbs brushed a slow circle on her sleeves. "Then I don't want to let go."

She smiled and stretched toward him for a kiss.

Lexi cleared her throat.

Gigi and Rory straightened, halting before their lips touched.

"Adorable," Lexi said flatly. "But we're done here."

Gigi looked around the ghost at the drawing Ken had done. The perpetrator had sunken, dark eyes with loose skin around his jaws and neck. A scar puckered the right side of his top lip. Dark locks of hair were strewn haphazardly about his head. Whoever he was, he'd pushed Lexi down the stairs and walked away, leaving her for dead. Gigi would find him, and he'd pay for his crimes.

Pulling out her phone, she took a picture of the drawing. At four feet of wide canvas, she couldn't take the artwork with her.

"I'll run it through the database on the off chance he's a prior offender. Ken, I need to take you home. Thanks for your help."

"Send me a copy. I'll circulate it with the museum security," Rory offered.

"That's a fantastic idea. Thank you."

Lexi floated between them and down the hall. "Okay. Okay. Enough with the mushy eyes. Just because I set the two of you up doesn't mean I should have to suffer through the awkward initial stages of your romance."

Rory gave Gigi a crooked grin. "I'll see you tonight?"

She couldn't help but smile in return. "I'm looking forward to it."

Between the gala, a would-be killer, and a ballroom full of priceless artifacts, she had a feeling tonight would change everything—one way or another.

Eight

Rory adjusted the black jacket of his tux. Anticipation--that had nothing to do with the display of Irish antiquities--swirled through him.

"Are you goin' to actually court the woman or skip that part and go straight to kissin'?"

"This is the twenty-first century, *Granda*. Kissing is part of courtship."

"You were a lot more cautious with the other women you've dated."

Rory look at the ghost of a man he called grandfather. He was a remote ancestor but calling him grandfather was a lot easier than adding an innumerable number of "Greats" before the title. Sometimes he used the more formal *Seanathair* to address him. "So far as I knew, none of the other women saw ghosts. I was cautious of the amount of time and emotion I was willing to invest in someone who might not accept all that I am."

"So, you think this lassie is your destiny?"

"I don't know about destiny. But she is my equal, and

that's enough for me to risk everything I've been holding back."

"Gigi Dunnigan. Has a nice ring to it."

Rory rolled his eyes. "Risking everything doesn't imply that I'm ready to propose to her. There will be a courtship—as you call it. There'll be a courtship—as you call it. Dates. Time. We'll see if we're actually compatible."

"Compatibility? The way you were pressin' lips together, one might think you were only in it for the romance."

"I want it all. Trust, compatibility, romance. I don't know if we have all that, but I'm willing to find out." He brushed his hair, styling it away from his face.

"Just don't go squanderin' your inheritance." His grandfather crossed his arms with a pout.

"Squander my inheritance?" Rory asked with amusement. "Is that what I've been doing? All these years I thought I was reassembling our ancestral heritage. I've only tripled our net worth."

"And you've done a fine job, so don't go makin' bags of it now."

"Aye, thanks for the vote of confidence." Rory grinned, wondering if Emmet's sour mood represented concern that a woman might replace him in Rory's life. He'd have to take steps to ensure that Emmet knew that wasn't the case.

His grandfather bit his lip. "I do hope you find love though. It can enrich your life in a way no sum of money can."

AFTER SHE CURLED her hair in loose ringlets, Gigi shimmied into an emerald gown and added silver earrings. She looked down at the handwritten note that had accompanied the delivered garment.

Gigi—

This dress reminded me of your eyes. I'd be honored if you considered wearing it to the gala.

Each petal on the shamrock
brings a wish your way.
Good health, good luck, and happiness
for today and every day.
—Rory

Her throat felt oddly tight as she folded the note. No one had ever bought her a dress before—much less one that actually fit who she was.

Clutching a pair of silver strap sandals with three-inch heels, she walked out of the bedroom into the kitchen where Lexi was waiting for her.

"You look stunning," Lexi marveled.

Gigi held up her heels and shook them at Lexi. "I'm wearing heels for a man. I hope you're happy."

"So happy." Her friend beamed.

"This doesn't feel right," Gigi complained. "I'm going to a party while you're languishing in an ICU bed."

"You can't fix me," Lexi said. "I want you to have this night. Seize the moment. Enjoy the company of a man who's smitten with you. You finally have someone who shares your gift—who can show you what a gift it is. And no matter what happens to me, promise me you'll have no regrets. Accept that you couldn't have done anything to prevent what happened to me. Sitting at my bedside, listening to the machines and watching me lie there like a limp noodle, won't change my outcome either."

Gigi blinked away tears, trying not to smear her makeup.

"Promise me," Lexi said more harshly.

"I promise." Gigi slipped on her heels. "I uploaded the

87

sketch of your perp into the database. It'll take time to run for a match, so I'll check back on it tomorrow."

"Stop working," Lexi scolded her. "Drop cop-mode for one night."

"Pieces keep swirling in my head," Gigi defended herself.

"What pieces?"

"Your attack right before the gala. Your missing employee key card. And a DHS alert that Felix Casale—international art thief—is in Chicago."

"You think the cat burglar will go after the museum?"

"Maybe, but here's what doesn't fit—Felix isn't known for violence, so your injury is uncharacteristic. I know art thieves, and I've studied his thefts. Also, your sketch doesn't match the vague descriptions we have of Felix."

"You know what it sounds like to me?" Lexi asked. "That you aren't going to solve this case tonight. So enjoy the gala like the date it's meant to be."

"I looked Rory up online," Gigi confessed.

"I'm surprised that's all you did. No background check?"

"Anyway. Did you know that, among other accolades, he trained through the Dublin Historical European Martial Arts Club and won a sword fighting tournament. Who fights with swords these days?"

"Apparently, handsome Irish gentlemen. Go make the most of this night. And don't make it an early one. Enjoy it. Turn the detective off, and work my case tomorrow."

"It's not a switch I can flip."

"I bet Rory can flip that switch." Lexi winked.

THE MUSEUM HAD BEEN DECORATED FESTIVELY with green tapestries along the walls and shimmering shamrocks dangling from the ceiling. An Irish band played lively music with fiddles, bagpipes, an Irish harp, an accordion, and a bodhran to accentuate the rhythm. Green mimosas—champagne, orange juice, and a splash of Blue Curacao—bubbled in slender glasses on trays before landing in the hands of delighted patrons.

Rory's relics, along with the museum's own Irish antiques, gleamed on display in various cases around the large room. Rory weaved around them and the small standing tables, stopping when people took an interest in the artifacts so he could explain the culture or history behind various pieces. He recognized most of them as he attempted to enthrall Chicago's elite —politicians, doctors, lawyers, business owners, and judges. This was, after all, a fundraiser. Tonight was about philanthropy, both for the museum itself as well as funding the Dunnigan Foundation which employed Irish men and women to excavate and search for artifacts both in the states and Ireland.

Irish culture in Chicago played a role in supporting such an event. After immigrants fled the country during the Irish famine in the 1840s, Chicago had become the fourth largest Irish city in America. Since then, they'd layered themselves into politics, religion, and public works. Irish churches contributed to the establishment of schools, orphanages, and hospitals.

With the cultural heritage, Irish art had become intricately woven into the city through architecture with renowned names like Martin A. Carr, James J. Eagan, and Alex Kirkland. Thomas A. O'Shaughnessy was famed for his Celtic revival art. Rory had a mix of Celtic art out for viewing—jewelry, pottery, and tapestries.

He scanned the crowd, searching for Gigi. He had wanted to pick her up and escort her to the fundraiser himself, but he'd needed to be at the event early and ensure the Irish display looked presentable. Because he wanted her to enjoy the night and not stand around waiting for festivities to start, he hadn't made the offer to bring her early.

Instead, he'd bought a dress for her and had it couriered over. The green was not only fitting for Saint Patrick's Day, but would match her eyes. He hoped she'd accept it as a gift and not misinterpret and think he was a controlling man.

Rory's breath hitched when he caught sight of Gigi in the green gown talking with Judge O'Malley. Glossy brown hair curled around her oval face. Her dress hugged every curve, and a sparkling silver bracelet and earrings polished the look.

Patrons stopped him several times during his trajectory to see her, but at last he circled around and came up behind her.

He whispered in her ear, "You look positively stunning, *a mhuirnín*." His lips were close to her ear as he spilled warm breath on her bare neck while calling her *my darling*.

When she turned around, her smile shone wide and brilliant. He'd never seen her whole face beaming with happiness. He wondered if he could take credit for some of that—she wasn't alone with her ghosts anymore.

"Won't you come dance with me?" he asked.

She looked around nervously as her smile faltered. "No one is dancing."

"That's because they need inspiration. And if I don't occupy myself with you in my arms, I'll not have a chance to spend any time with you, owing to the constant cycle of socializing."

"Well, far be it for me to interfere with your plans to take a break from socializing, but I had readied my next toast for our next drink."

He smiled to think she wanted to keep their exchange of

toasts going. And he adored that Gigi didn't care what other people thought. If she didn't want to date a man, she'd show him her badge as a deterrent. If she needed to enter the mall to pick up her uncle in his pajamas, she wouldn't hesitate. If she needed to defuse a dangerous situation with a dozen onlookers videoing the event, she would march up and take control of the scene. If she wanted to be the only person dancing in a crowded room, she would let Rory lead her to an open section of floor near the band.

Despite being different and growing up feeling cursed or crazy, she had persevered and established her independence and strong personality.

The band played a slow, sweet ballad, and they swayed together.

"What's your toast, Detective?"

> *"May your pockets be heavy*
> *May your heart be light.*
> *May good luck follow you through morning*
>   *and night."*

He leaned in closer and pressed a light kiss to her lips. "If you can't close the toast with a drink, you need to seal it with a kiss. It'd be bad luck otherwise."

"Is that so?" She chuckled.

He said,

> *"Like the warmth of the sun*
> *and the light of the its rays,*
> *may the luck of the Irish*
> *shine bright on your days.*

I'm glad you came. I was starting to worry," Rory

confessed. He didn't want to imply she arrived late, but he had expected to see her sooner.

She arched up and gave him a kiss. "Toast safely sealed."

"Admittedly," she began, "I struggled for a little while deciding if I should come. Lexi had to encourage me. It still feels awkward sharing happy moments with you when I don't know what else to do to help her."

Other people started dancing around them to the music.

"You feel guilty."

"Yes, her predicament led me to this—to us. Whatever it is, it feels like the start of something special. But it feels wrong to enjoy life when she can't."

"I see. And I'm guessing she told you to come?"

"Yes. I've done everything I can think to do. I walked the museum. I inspected the security footage as much as I could until Theo interrupted. I uploaded the image of the violent offender for facial recognition and circulated his image in the department as a person of interest..." her voice trailed.

The head of museum security approached Rory, and the pair of them stopped dancing.

"Mac?" Rory said.

In a low voice of discretion, Mac said, "Mr. Dunnigan, I know you told me to text or call if this happened, but I knew you were here tonight so I decided to find you directly. Somebody used Lexi Blackwell's badge to access the vault."

A boom and crackling noise startled everyone. Gazes turned skyward where a bursting rainbow of glittering color lit the sky.

Rory narrowed his eyes at the skylight. He hadn't requested fireworks, and although he hadn't micromanaged the entire Saint Patrick's Day event, he certainly would have known about fireworks. A cold chill swept down his back as he looked around at the delighted people in the crowded room. They were awestruck by the display.

By the *distraction*.

The fireworks would provide an excellent disturbance for a thief looking to make his move. As a thief himself, Rory knew how to spot the ploys of one.

He met Gigi's gaze, and at the same moment they said, "It's a diversion."

"I'll check the display," Rory said, thinking mostly of the prized cross. It was secured under a glass case, but such a thing could be bypassed.

Gigi turned to the security guard. "Mac, take me to the cameras. Show me the one with the location of where Lexi's card was accessed."

Rory gave Gigi's hand one last squeeze before he rushed to the showroom.

When he reached the circular chamber with high ceiling, a few people loitered, gazing at the swords, pottery, and the cross —the jeweled cross Rory had stolen from another thief. The artifacts were showcased under golden spotlights, with some on pedestals and others on shelves along the walls. The swords were mounted next to a large burgundy tapestry bearing Celtic symbols.

"You're missing the fireworks," Rory announced with a forced smile as he gestured for the spectators to leave.

All of them walked out, save one.

Rory's blood ran hot and cold at once at the sight of a tall man in a tuxedo with his back to him as he stood facing the cross.

"Felix," Rory practically hissed the name.

Nine

Gigi followed Mac toward the security room. "Where's the rest of your crew?"

"When Lexi's badge triggered, so did about half a dozen other alarms. My men are spread out." The security guard swiped his badge to unlock the door to the security offices.

Gigi stepped into the hallway with him and walked down to the viewing room.

She contemplated the alarms triggering. They were motion sensitive, but nothing specified that motion had to be made by a human. An intruder could have planted robots or drones to trigger the security devices by hovering too close to objects on display.

Gigi's gaze quickly scanned the video footage—Mayan exhibit, Greek and Roman exhibit, prehistoric exhibit, hallways, offices, and more.

"There." She pointed to a man in a waiter's suit walking down a corridor. She knew that man—had seen a four-foot sketch of his face.

Lexi's attacker.

"Where is this?"

"Employee hallway."

"Anything valuable in there?"

"Yes. A lot in storage. But look here!" He pointed to a screen where Rory faced-off against a man in a tux.

They stood alone together in the display room of the more prized Irish artifacts—many of which belonged to Rory. The man tucked a golden cross from the center display into his tuxedo.

Gigi glanced back and forth between screens—which man to go after? Rory and his opponent each took a sword—a claideb—down from a wall display and faced off.

"Does that room seal?" she asked.

"Yes, but Mr. Dunnigan—"

"Seal it off until you can send a team there. We'll have to trust that Rory's fencing training will keep him alive until then."

With the press of a button, a metal lattice work descended, jailing the two men inside the room.

"You need to shut down the rest of the museum. We don't know if these are the only two thieves." Gigi turned and left. "I'm going after the other one."

"I'll help you. You'll need badge access." He began to follow as he barked orders into his radio but fell several paces behind her.

She ran in her heels while hiking up her long dress. "Lexi, I need a navigator."

The ghost appeared in front of her. "Follow me! This is exciting. We're like Tango and Cash. Batman and Robin."

"More like Casper and Mantha."

Lexi snorted. "That makes you zombie girl. My analogy was better."

"Is he armed?" Gigi asked.

"No."

Good. Because Gigi wasn't either.

When Mac caught up to her, he swiped his card and led them through an employee door. They slowed their pace to walk down the corridor. Gigi listened for the intruder's footfalls but heard nothing.

Mac said, "We have two large rooms down here filled with valuables. High priced items are behind a vault requiring two-person, two key access."

The walls on either side of them became glass partitions. Lighted tables sat at the forefront where items could be viewed or cleaned. Behind them stretched rows of shelves with catalogued valuables.

From one of the rooms, a streak of black launched at them. Gigi pivoted away on instinct. Lexi's attacker barreled into Mac, the impact so hard it drove both men straight through the glass wall in a deafening crash.

Mac took the brunt of the force and remained on the ground as the attacker rolled to his feet. He withdrew a knife and slashed in Gigi's direction.

She jumped back, practically twisting her ankle. "Lexi," she said through gritted teeth, "we consider twelve-inch blades armed."

"Oh. I just thought you were asking if he had a gun."

Gigi retreated a few calculated steps as the man crunched over broken glass to advance on her.

She considered talking—explaining that the police were on their way and the museum was locked down—but his contorted face already said he knew he was cornered. Cornered animals didn't negotiate.

As he lunged toward her, she yanked a fire extinguisher off the wall. Using it as a shield, she blocked three of his quick slashes. On the last one, his hand hit the metal cylinder rather than the knife.

With a snarl of pain, he retreated a step. He seemed to realize he wasn't facing an easy opponent.

He let out an animalistic growl. "You're the cop from the mall shooting."

"That's me. And you're under arrest." Gigi's heart pounded as hard as it had running through the mall the other day. Alone, she faced a man wielding a knife, and, while she had hand-to-hand combat training and had been in fights, this situation was especially dangerous. She squared off in a narrow space with a cornered, wild animal holding a deadly blade. She had no armor and no weapon.

"Oh. You're not taking me in. I'm never going back."

When he launched another offensive attack, she blocked the knife twice but saw the follow-up punch too late to dodge it.

His fist struck her jaw, and pain exploded through the side of her face. The fact that she was still standing told her he hadn't been close enough for the full power of a knock-out, even though her jaw registered the worst blow it had ever taken.

A glint of steel flashed as the attacker wasted no time taking advantage of her momentary stunned state.

Her arms were growing weak, but she blocked two more blows—the last one angled so the knife slid down the smooth metal of the extinguisher and sliced into her hand.

White-hot pain flared, and warm blood slicked the handle, but she refused to let go. Before he could swing again, she lunged toward him, the metal colliding with his nose.

He cried out, stumbling back.

The distance between them gave her the opportunity to

pull the release, aim the device, and sweep a torrent of compressed nitrogen gas over him.

Clutching his bleeding nose, he blindly stumbled backward and slipped on the unstable surface of shattered glass.

Gigi dropped the canister onto his knife hand. He released the blade, crying out in agony at the shattered bones.

She rushed to Mac, placing two fingers on his carotid artery and breathing a sigh of relief when she found a strong pulse. She pulled the handcuffs off his belt and secured the criminal's uninjured hand to the metal beam that had once held the glass partition in place.

After tearing a long strip of green fabric from her dress, she wrapped her hand to stop the bleeding and unclipped the radio running from Mac's waist to his shoulder, speaking into it. "This is Detective Montgomery. Mac is unconscious. Perp is male, mid-forties, armed with a knife and handcuffed to a support beam in the basement storage facility. I need medical and backup."

The man on the floor wouldn't be able to pick his cuffs with the fingers of his right hand broken, but given time, he might be able to kick the beam into giving way. Hopefully, the museum security would arrive before that could happen. She couldn't stay and watch the pair of them. She needed to check on Rory.

"How's Rory?" she asked Lexi.

"Holding his own in a sword fight."

"Take me to him."

RORY AND FELIX'S gaze landed on the claideb swords almost simultaneously. Rory had found them on a dig outside Tralee two years ago and had added them to his collection.

Felix unleashed a feral smile. No. A *feline* smile, Rory decided—part challenge, part haughty amusement.

"Shall we?" Rory offered, reaching for a blade.

"A gentleman's duel? I accept," Felix said in his polished English accent.

As they squared off, the security gate lowered. Rory had cut off Felix's escape route so he had no way of slipping under the gate before it sealed them in the room together.

Rory returned the smile—equally challenging and haughty—as he adjusted his grip. Wooden hilts had replaced the original horns that hadn't survived over the hundreds of years since their construction.

Amusement dancing in his eyes, Felix made the first jab with the two-foot long double blade of battered bronze.

Rory blocked.

They fought—swords clashing as they moved, almost dance-like, around the room, careful to leave the priceless artifacts undisturbed.

Their blows contained no maliciousness, only practiced motions. They were rivals with opposing objectives—Rory to preserve Irish heritage, and Felix to preserve his reputation ... and bank account. But neither men were truly violent.

"Your hired help threw a woman down the stairs, Felix." Rory parried, then struck.

Felix blocked. "I know." He frowned. "I do feel awful about that. I won't be using his services again. Good help—well, you know—it truly is hard to find."

Rory unintentionally winged his elbow slightly too far and bumped a tripartite carinated potter piece with faded red paint. It teetered and almost fell, but Felix caught it with his free hand. He gave Rory a scolding look as if to suggest he'd just deducted style points.

Rory chuckled, but didn't use the distraction to his advantage. He waited until Felix had stabilized the vase before clashing blades again.

"There won't be a next time," Rory said, "because you're trapped and about to be arrested."

It was Felix's turn to laugh, and Rory understood why. As a master thief and chameleon, the man wouldn't be contained long. Rory gauged how he felt about that. He didn't want to lose the challenge of such a fun adversary. With Felix still lose in the world, Rory would stay at the top of his game.

"You could join me," Felix offered. "The world is our oyster, and we'd never be as sloppy as the man who hurt the museum worker."

They fought around the empty pedestal where the cross had sat.

"Why don't *you* join *me*?" Rory countered, slightly winded now. "You would have the satisfaction of retrieving pieces for a good cause."

"Hmm. Money is a good cause. My reputation would be irrevocably tarnished if I began doing charity work."

"Tarnished or polished?"

"Sometimes the best pieces are ones never fully restored."

With a grating noise, the gate began to lift.

"Chicago PD! Put the swords down! You're under arrest." Three men in blue stood with weapons drawn.

Felix lowered the blade, then held it up as an offering of surrender to Rory. With a mischievous glint in his eye, he said, "Until we meet again, my friend."

He bowed as Rory accepted the sword. Rory reached into the other man's tux and withdrew the cross from his inside pocket.

When the police rushed in to arrest Felix, Rory turned away and replaced the swords on their mounts. He didn't want to watch the great Felix Casale carted off in cuffs.

Turning back around, he saw Gigi talking to various officers and security guards. She seemed to be filling them in on the night's activities.

Apparently, he wasn't the only one who'd been in a skirmish. Her hair was a ball of brown tangles, and her dress was torn. A large red welt discolored her jaw, and a bandage of green fabric wrapped around her left hand.

"You're staring," Lexi said as she appeared beside him.

"Seems she put the dress I bought her to good use," he said. "She's magnificent. Is she hurt?"

"Nothing a little ice and skin glue can't fix."

"Did she catch your assailant?"

"Of course she did." Lexi beamed like a proud friend, but her ghost form began to flicker and fade.

"Don't you have a body to get back to?" he asked gently.

"Yeah," she sniffed, "If I don't make it, you'll look after her."

"She hardly needs looking after, but, yes, she's not ridding herself of me. But you're not going anywhere. Go to the body calling to you and come back to us whole."

Lexi nodded, fear in her eyes as she vanished. Rory didn't know what would happen to Lexi now, but he hoped for the best. He stared at the empty air where she'd been, the last echo of her presence prickling over his skin.

Ten

Gigi hadn't had a chance to check on Rory. She had, after all, locked him in a room with a criminal and sharp, pointy objects. He might be furious with her, but she had to delegate first. Mac and the assailant needed medical care. Patrons needed to be safely escorted out of the museum. Felix needed to be taken to the station to be booked and processed.

And where had Lexi disappeared to?

"Gigi?"

She turned to see her father in uniform walking toward her.

"Dad?" She straightened automatically, suddenly feeling like a kid playing dress-up rather than the detective who'd been barking orders a few minutes ago. The tattered green gown and bruises didn't help.

He stopped short, looking like he wanted to hug her but not wanting to undermine her authority.

She opted to keep the interaction strictly professional as the best way to maintain her composure. "Felix Casale tried a heist here tonight. He hired someone to steal Lexi's badge three days ago and set up distractions in order to make a play for Mr. Dunnigan's cross."

She had seen Felix escorted outside to a black and white. Rory had disappeared with a security entourage shortly after that.

"You're okay?" her father asked.

"I'm okay." She abstained from flexing her fingers so as to avoid opening the wound on her hand. She had no idea what her face looked like, but her jaw pleaded for ice with every word she spoke.

"You did good. We'll take it from here."

She nodded, relieved. She wanted a shower and a warm bed. She was—what was the Irish phrase?—knackered. Shivering, she took one last look around before walking toward the exit.

A gentle hand touched her shoulder. "Detective?"

The rich Irish voice had her instantly warming. She turned to meet soft brown eyes.

"I'm sorry," Rory began, "I've been trying to get to you for the last half hour. I've a private physician on standby outside near my driver. Please allow him to examine you and help—at least for my peace of mind. I'd go with you, but I need to see that the exhibit's properly secured."

After everything she'd been through and her level of exhaustion, she appreciated the offer of help and wouldn't fight out of any childish desire to maintain a show of strength and independence.

"You're not mad at me for locking you in with Felix?" she asked.

He bent and gave her a brief kiss. "It worked. And I suspect you already knew the thief has a reputation for nonviolent interactions."

"Yes. And I saw you reach for the swords—a weapon you have some experience with."

He gave her another kiss. "I'll see you as soon as I can." He moved to gently touch his lips to her tender jaw before pulling her into his arms.

RORY DIDN'T FINISH at the museum until two a.m. During his work, he'd taken a call from the physician who said he had Gigi's permission to tell Rory her cuts had been treated and she would heal quickly. He'd also received a text message from his driver, William, informing him that Gigi had him take her to the hospital to check on her friend.

Before Rory left the museum, he caught up with Theo. "Any word on Mac?"

Theo removed his glasses and rubbed a baggy pair of eyes. "Concussion. He's admitted for overnight observation. His brother is checking in on him."

"Good. I'll touch base with you tomorrow."

"Certainly, Mr. Dunnigan."

When Rory emerged outside, he was surprised to see his driver parked out front.

"I saw her safely home," William assured Rory.

"Did she mention how her friend in the ICU is faring?"

"She said she's improved, and the breathing tube is out. She also said there was talk of her moving out of the ICU tomorrow."

Emmet appeared, hands on hips and a twinkle in his eyes. "You did good, lad. So did your fair lady. Everyone will recover."

Rory winked at Emmet as he clasped William's shoulder,

relief sweeping through him. "We'll call that a Saint Patrick's Day miracle."

THE NEXT MORNING, Gigi drove up to the hospital to see Lexi. She'd slept in later than she'd planned, but the night's activities had drained her. At least she was out of her dress and heels and back in blue jeans and a sweater.

TJ texted her, *Hope that green dress wasn't a rental. You're not getting your money back.*

She snorted. Apparently, she'd made the news again. Trust her brother to reduce attempted art theft and a knife fight to a wardrobe malfunction.

Rather than fire back with a defensive retort, she opted for offensive, *You need to tell me what's going on between you and Lexi.*

When she'd dropped by to check on Lexi last night, TJ had been there. Gigi had felt too exhausted to interrogate him about his level of concern over Lexi's health.

TJ didn't reply to her text.

When she entered the ICU room with two coffees, Lexi was sitting up in bed with her mother in the chair beside her. Her friend looked far better awake and off life support, but her coloring was still pale.

"Oh, Gigi!" Mrs. Blackwell stood, smile beaming. "I'll step out and let you girls talk."

As she exited the room, Gigi set the coffee on a small bedside table.

"Almond milk and honey?" Lexi asked hopefully.

"You know I've got your back." Gigi practically deflated into the chair.

Although Lexi's breathing tube had been removed last

night, she'd still been in no condition for conversation. Now that she was sitting up and talking, Gigi's anxiety ebbed.

Lexi gave a moan of delight as she sipped the drink. "Mmm. You are a true best friend."

"Don't ever scare me like that again."

Lexi smirked. "Go ahead and ask. You know you want to."

"Ask what?"

Lexi gave her an I-know-you-better-than-yourself look.

Gigi leaned back in her seat, turning the plastic lid of her paper coffee cup in a slow circle. "How much do you remember?"

"How much of what do I remember?" She wriggled her eyebrows.

Gigi grinned. "How much of being a ghost do you remember?"

She smiled. "Bits and pieces. Helping you solve my case. Uncle Ken. Your pretty silver heels. Rory making dreamy eyes at you. Yeah, kind of like that." She gestured to the door.

Gigi followed her gaze to see Rory standing in the doorway.

"Hi." She set her cup down and stood.

He entered. "Lexi, good to see you looking bonny."

"Not sure about bonny, but I'll take this over having one foot in the grave."

He set an envelope on the table. "The museum staff sent a get-well card. Apparently, they'd saved you a slice of the shamrock cake, but the night shift ate it."

"Figures," she grumbled.

"Dinner at my place—the three of us—when you're well enough," Gigi announced.

"Uh. No. I don't do third wheels. But I'd be up for Thirsty Thursday." Lexi took another sip of her coffee.

"I could bring Uncle Ken to dinner. He'll make it a four-wheeler."

"I do like your quirky uncle. He's fun."

"The four of us then. My place."

"I'll cook," Rory offered, reaching out and taking Gigi's uninjured hand.

A tingling warmth spread from his touch up through her arm and across her chest. She couldn't believe she'd found someone with the same gift she had who also enjoyed art and history. And he was an all-around nice guy.

"Ugh. Okay, you two," Lexi said. "Get a room. This one's taken."

Gigi turned back to her friend.

"Out, out." Lexi waved at them. "I really do want to a rest a bit."

Gigi nodded, picking up her coffee and heading toward the door with Rory. "Call me when you want company."

As they waited at the end of the hall for the elevator, Rory asked, "Can I interest you in breakfast?"

"You and your meals. Yeah, my place." She grinned, still holding his hand.

He arched an eyebrow. "I've earned enough trust for that?"

"Yes, you have. Although, based on last night's dress delivery, you already know where I live. I am sorry about the dress."

"If anything I ever buy you can be used in time of peril, don't apologize."

They took the elevator down and walked toward his waiting car.

He stopped her short of reaching it and turned toward her. "I want your trust, Gigi. All of it. But you need to know one more thing about me, and the cop in you won't like it."

Her body went still. The detective in her braced for the

worst, while the woman who'd watched him risk his life last night wanted to tell him she didn't need to hear it.

He continued, "I'm all things you've seen—art dealer and philanthropist. But because of the ghost connections I have, I can also learn about lost or stolen artifacts. The lost ones aren't a problem." He dragged a hand through his hair. "The stolen ones are trickier. Sometimes, to put them back where they belong...I have to take them first."

He met her gaze head-on. "Which makes me, technically, a thief."

She stayed still, the beats of silence seeming loud.

"I learned from one of the best," he added quietly.

"Felix?"

"Yes. I laid a trap and caught him some years ago. In exchange for his freedom, he agreed to teach me. I was his apprentice for several years until he tired of my insistence that we only steal to reclaim stolen artifacts."

"You became a thief of thieves."

"Yes," he said hesitantly. "With the exception that most people I stole from bought the items off the black market and didn't steal the items themselves."

As she digested this bit of information, Rory looked as though he was bracing himself for rejection. Her training screamed words like felony and confession; her heart threw back images of him cooking her dinner, grounding her when the world tilted, standing between priceless relics and a master thief.

"Can you give me some time to decide how I feel about this?"

He pulled her in closer. "As much as time you need. So long we're still having that breakfast."

She smiled. "Yes, we are." She stretched up and gave him brief kiss on the cheek.

∾

SIX MONTHS LATER

"It's gorgeous," Gigi said as they stood in Rory's showroom at his home in Dublin.

"Thank you for helping me assemble the pieces." Rory took her hand as they admired the collar of a knight of the Order of Saint Patrick. The thick gold chain rested on a black felt mannequin.

"We're a team." She squeezed his hand, blissfully amazed by their whirlwind trips around the world over the last several months to collect all of the pieces with the help of Rory's great grandfather.

She'd used all of her vacation time from the force to travel with Rory. And she'd spent the time on planes and trains to submit her resume for art crimes investigator to several private insurance companies. Thwarting the famous Felix Casale would hopefully boost her potential for a job in the private sector, though it wasn't her fault he'd managed to escape custody before ever being booked for the attempted theft of Rory's cross. Somewhere out there, the cat burglar was licking his wounds and plotting. She'd almost be disappointed if he weren't.

"We are a team. And I'd like to make it official." He turned toward her and extended a four-leaf clover to her.

Puzzled, she took the shamrock.

"I fell in love with you that night at the Saint Patrick's Day gala," he told her. "You're brave, resilient, dedicated, and compassionate. And of course, beautiful. So beautiful. I've thanked my lucky stars to have you in my life every day since then. And, no matter where our travels take us—separate or together, for work or for pleasure—I want to come home to you." He knelt down on one knee and presented her with a ring. The white gold had a central diamond surrounded on either side by Celtic trinity knots.

Gigi gasped.

"Will you marry me, Gigi Montgomery. You're my rainbow and pot of gold all twined into one. *A chuisle, a chroi.* My pulse, my heart."

"Yes." Her vision swam with tears.

Before Rory, she'd never dared imagine the possibilities which awaited. Once she realized the gift she had in the paranormal, she was free to explore these possibilities and travel. Rory had been a gift as well. He'd set her free from her own inhibitions and fears.

"I love you," she said on a half sob.

He slipped the ring on her finger as he stood. "*Mo shiorghra,*" he whispered. "My eternal love."

She arched up to seal her promise of love with a kiss. The magic of the moment stole her breath away as his embrace and sensual kiss sent a euphoric wave of heat through her entire body.

"*Mo shiorghra,*" she echoed.

<<<THE END>>>

***** QUICK NOTE FROM THE AUTHOR *****

READY FOR ANOTHER sweet and magical romantic suspense? There are so many delights to enjoy! Keep scrolling for the first chapter in the next book.

IN BOXED SETS

INDIVIDUAL BOOKS

Romancing the Spirit Series #1
Sadie's Spirit / Willow's Windfall
Cassie's Chase / Phoebe's Pharaoh
Vanessa's Valentine / Autumn's Angel
Romancing the Spirit Series #2
Carol's Christmas / Allison's Alibi
Gracelynn's Genie / Michelle's Miracle
Heather's Hero / Chloe's Cupid
Romancing the Spirit Series #3
Sabrina's Storm / Jenny's Justice
Stella's Star / Gigi's Gift
Phoenix's Phantom / Fiona's Freedom

THE CHRISTMAS COLLECTION

Other Books by CB Samet

Looking for more romantic suspense with more action and sizzle? How about with an urban fantasy twist? Check out my supernatural adventures...

The Shadow Guardians Trilogy

Urban fantasy Norse Mythology Adventure

Get *Raven's Flight, a prequel novella* for FREE. In my newsletter, you'll learn about me, special discounts, and new releases.

Raven's Flight, prequel novella

Raine Down, Book 1

Rosalyn's Run, novella

Storm Surge, Book 2

Anka's Orb, novella

Sky Fall, Book 3

Olympian Awakenings Trilogy

Urban fantasy Greek Mythology Adventure

Grab the prequel exclusively HERE.

Stone Hearts

Winds of Destiny

Flame and Shadow

The Rider Files

Romantic Suspense Thrillers

Meridian File / Masters File / Box Set 1

McMillan File / Maltisse File / Box Set 2

Storm File / Sullivan File / Box Set 3

Sharp File / Sizani File / Box Set 4

Rivera File / Rucker File / Box Set 5

Richmond File / Redwood File / Box Set 6

Atlas File / Angel File / Box Set 7

Buy 4book box sets direct from author and save 10%

Payhip. Use code E152M0GZG4

∽

The Dr. Whyte Adventure Novels

Thriller Series

Black Gold

Whyte Knight

Gray Horizon

∽

Love action/adventure and strong female leads in a fantasy world? Check out my other genre:

The Avant Champion Fantasy Series

The Avant Champion: Rising

Malakai: An Avant Champion Origin of Malos Story (prequel)

The Avant Champion: Honor

The Avant Champion: Ashes

Brothers' Bond: An Avant Champion Malakai Story

The Avant Champion: Conquest

Isabel: An Avant Champion novelette

The Avant Champion: Redeem

Dear Reader

If you enjoyed this book and want to know about future releases by CB SAMET, you can CLICK HERE to sign up for my mailing list! I promise I won't spam you. I only send an email when I have a new book released, giveaways, or special discounts. You can also unsubscribe at any time.

Keep reading for a sample chapter of the next novella!

Also, as an independent author, I rely heavily on readers to spread the word about books they've read. If you enjoyed this story, kindly let others know by posing a brief comment on social media or leave a review where you purchased it.

Thank you for reading,

Phoenix's Phantom

SAMPLE CHAPTER

Phoenix crept down the gray stone staircase, using the flashlight on her mobile phone to light the way. The cavernous underground room spread out before her. Without the beam from her phone, she would have been in total darkness, yet, she still would have known her way around. She'd wandered beneath the theater so many times, her feet knew the number of steps descending into the circular chamber.

Each time she came here, she marveled at the mosaic pattern of light and dark blue stones on the floor, large gray columns, and overhanging archway. But what drew her here time and again wasn't the solitude and isolation of the room; it was the music she heard within it—breathtaking and beautiful music sung by a ghost haunting this chamber.

She'd found the large room while following the sound of a baritone from her backstage changing room one day. The voice had led her down the hallway to a storage closet where she'd discovered a hidden door, behind which a set of stairs plunged into blackness.

Now, standing once again in the large chamber and surrounded in chilled air and the smell of old stone, she began singing *Come What May* from the musical *Moulin Rouge*. She didn't have the voice projection or classical training required for opera, but that suited her perfectly since she preferred the exchange of dialogue and song in musicals.

The acoustics of the room took her version of the melody and reverberated the sound off the walls, echoing the tune into something both eerie and beautiful. She'd learned she could sing almost any Broadway tune in order to summon the spirit lingering down here, if the ghostly voice hadn't already initiated the singing prior to her arrival.

Before she reached the second verse, she heard his voice, warm and mesmerizing as liquid gold. Awe filled her as his voice enveloped her. Their voices entwined seamlessly, and she imagined a soft guitar playing in the background.

She didn't know the phantom's name. They had no interaction beyond singing. She didn't even know what he looked like or how old he'd been when he died. Not knowing his name, she had given him one—Gaston.

Phoenix had known the gift of seeing or hearing ghosts would manifest at some point in her life since her father and sister had the gift, and she was pleasantly surprised to be visited by a singing ghost, if a little distraught after discovering that he only ever sang.

When their duet concluded, she stayed quiet for a moment, letting Gaston pick the next song. He began to serenade her with *Some Enchanted Evening*. Even though the *South Pacific* song was a male solo, she joined him.

This time, something felt different. His voice grew louder and edgier, overpowering hers. She stopped singing and listened. Something in the urgency of his tone and the caution in his voice conveyed danger. Unlike the many other occasions she'd come down here and enjoyed fun or peaceful duets, this time she sensed he was warning her about something.

What hazards could possibly lay ahead of her? She sang musicals at a theater in New York City. Fear of an injury benching her always lingered in the back of her mind, but she didn't do anything hazardous outside of the workplace. Her only other fear was laryngitis. Perhaps he was cautioning her to stay away from him, but that made no sense; he was a singing ghost. What was more harmless than him?

"I don't know what you're trying to tell me," she said with frustration into the empty room when Gaston finished the song. "If you can sing, you can speak. Tell me who you are. Tell me why you're here."

She'd asked him a dozen times before for more information, but since he'd never given her an answer in the past, she didn't expect one this time. Disappointed in the ghost's continued lack of response, she turned and climbed the stairs back to the closet near the backstage offices of the theater.

Lance packed several bags of luggage in the loft bedroom where he'd spent the last week on vacation. He relocated several times a year for his work in the entertainment business, but this time he was excited to return to New York for a more permanent position.

Behind him, the creak of footsteps coming up the stairs to his room caught his attention. His door slowly swung open.

"Hello, Nana." Even without looking, he knew she approached by the slow footsteps.

"You're off again," she said wistfully.

Although he'd already told her he had a new job in the US, he explained again, "It's a theater in New York. They need a new stage director."

She leaned against the doorframe, her lined face carrying a soft smile. "You were happier when you were the one on stage." She crossed her arms. "And the more time you spend in America, the more you start to sound like a North American."

He turned to look at her. "I'm happy. I enjoyed the stage, but I found I have stronger talents elsewhere. Who was it that said 'follow your talents not your dreams?' Besides, I'm rewarded every time one of the young talents I mentor succeeds."

"I wish you didn't have to go for such long stretches. I'm an old woman, you know. My days are numbered."

He walked over and kissed her cheeks, first one side and then the other. "Everyone's days are numbered, Nana. And you've been using that line for the better part of two decades." Still, he would miss her and wasn't sure when his next holiday would bring him back to her. He squeezed her arm.

Her warm smile faltered, her spine going rigid.

He pulled back. "What's wrong?"

"You do need to go." Her gaze turned distant. "She needs you."

Lance swallowed hard. He didn't like that look in his grandmother's eyes, but he knew it all too well. As long as he'd known her, she'd had an uncanny ability to predict the future. A rough outline and nothing precise, but often right regardless. Everyone in the family knew to heed her warnings. She'd once explained that spirits spoke to her, telling her of luck and danger. While Lance found this an insufficient explanation, he knew enough to pay attention when she had one of her premonitions.

"Who needs me, Nana?" he asked gently.

The one whose song you never finished. She's always needed you. But this time there's danger."

"What danger?" The hairs on his arms rose.

"You'll know. Keep on your toes." She blinked away the distant gaze before patting his cheek as though she hadn't just told him something terrible was on the horizon.

Lance thought about his grandmother's many predictions —when Tommy fell off his roof and broke his arm; when Aunt Georgia wore high heels to Mave's wedding and twisted her ankle.

But they weren't always accurate. When he'd left for a performance position in New York years ago, Nana had told him the spirits ordained he would find his match, the woman he would spend his life sharing dreams and happiness with. That hadn't happened. Or maybe it could have, but fate had stolen the opportunity.

Nothing could be done about those events now, though he'd never stopped fantasizing about what might have been under different circumstances.

He zipped up his bags and turned back to his grandmother. "Video chat once a week. Okay?"

"You're going to do great. Go break a leg." She winked at him.

"Pull yourself together, Harry." Bowman sat beside the fidgeting old man on a bench in Central Park.

With trembling hands, Harry dabbed a handkerchief to his moist brow despite the cool fall breeze. "This wasn't supposed to happen."

"Accidents happen," Bowman tried to reassure him.

If the man didn't calm down, he would give himself a

stroke or heart attack right here on the lawn. Bowman wasn't about to lock lips and perform CPR on anyone, even if Harry was willing to sell the theater to him.

But Harry didn't own the old building yet; his brother did.

"It wasn't an accident," Harry countered, his voice thick with misery. His gaze darted around as if he was afraid the two of them were being watched. "I killed a man. I meant to poison Cillian—something I at least thought would be an act of mercy given his state of health—but the wrong man ate the medication."

"A tragic accident," Bowman insisted in as gentle a tone as he could, but honestly, how much longer would he have to listen to Harry's self-flagellation and blathering?

"You could turn yourself in," Bowman suggested, as if Harry had simply failed to parallel park correctly instead of poisoned the wrong person.

No one suspected wrongful death in the man Harry was referring to, but if Harry turned himself in, the scandal might disrupt Cillian's life enough he would be willing to sell the theater. Bowman doubted he would get so lucky.

Harry shook his head violently as he stared, hunched over, at the ground. "I'd die in jail. I'm done. I can't conspire like this anymore."

Bowman scowled at the implication that some fault lay with him. He'd never told Harry to kill his own brother; he'd merely discussed how the money Harry would make from the sale of Cillian's building would take care of his debts and unburden his children. If Harry chose to take action, Bowman couldn't be held responsible, even if he'd planted the seed and reaped the benefit.

Sure, Bowman manipulated people's thoughts, but their

actions were still subject to free will. The responsibility and consequences lay solely with the physical perpetrator.

He shifted his gaze across the park to Sheep Meadow where people threw balls or lounged on towels, soaking up the early autumn rays. His lips thinned in disdain. He was a man of ambition and achievement, not a sheep lazily grazing on wasted leisure time.

Bowman needed the deed in Harry's possession since his stodgy older brother refused to sell the run-down theater as he clung to some philanthropic desire to preserve the arts. Unlike his brother, Harry saw reason and was willing to sell—even though he was a basket case at this particular moment. And apparently capable of murder.

A heavy finality settled in Harry's tone as he pushed up from the bench with his cane. "I won't be a part of this anymore." In slow, frail steps, he ambled away down the walking path.

Bowman didn't follow. If he'd thought to record the conversation, a murder charge on Cillian's brother might be damaging enough to ruin him—except that it might also earn him public sympathy and help him.

Bowman couldn't enlist Harry's help if he was going to fall apart at the first stumbling block. However, Harry would still be willing to sell the theater to Bowman if Cillian was forced to surrender it. For this reason, Bowman needed to maintain a cordial relationship with Harry.

As for nudging the theater out of Cillian's grasp, Bowman would need to get more creative. New York didn't need to cling to another floundering theater, and the high-rise condominium he could put there would be infinitely more profitable and fulfill a societal need for residential space.

Bowman needed eyes and ears inside the theater to help

him create the right opportunity. If he couldn't financially undermine the owner through the brother, perhaps some other tragedy could hasten the timeline to foreclosure. Part of the key to Bowman's success was always having a back-up plan.

<<<CONTINUE READING PHEONIX'S PHANTOM>>>

www.ingramcontent.com/pod-product-compliance
Lightning Source LLC
Chambersburg PA
CBHW022030170626
46808CB00003B/1130